To Cast an Iron Shadow

Muneer Barkatullah

iUniverse, Inc.
Bloomington

To Cast an Iron Shadow

iUniverse books may be ordered through booksellers or by contacting:

iUniverse
1663 Liberty Drive
Bloomington, IN 47403
www.iuniverse.com
1-800-Authors (1-800-288-4677)

ISBN: 978-1-4620-0522-2 (sc)
ISBN: 978-1-4620-0605-2 (ebk)

Library of Congress Control Number: 2011903928

Printed in the United States of America

iUniverse rev. date: 3/18/2011

Dedicated to my son Noah

1

December 18, 1973

The lights of Islamabad illuminated the surrounding hills, and drew weary travelers like moths to a flame. Faisal Mosque was the crown jewel, centrally located within the heart, perfectly dissecting streets and homes. The city itself was planned much more meticulously than its ancient counterpart cities to the south.

The day had been unforgiving and relentless for Mohammed. Requests, denials, and extensions had taken their toll on the humble man. He had been summoned to a convention on the further development for the streets and cities of Pakistan. Mohammed was already a prominent architect and planner for Pakistan, his presence at the convention only enhanced the countries views of what was to be built. He had already given the city of Karachi his life's work and the people adored him for it. He was a refreshing presence in a city that was struggling to find an identity, and a city that was determined to break free from its backward dealings.

His presence at the convention was a bit odd, because it was his voice that originally stood against outlining a city such as Islamabad upon shifting Earth plates and fault lines. It was dangerous, and although there had not been an earthquake for over a hundred years, Mohammed was not as short sighted as those with deep pockets. As prominent as his rejection was to the undecided, he was among scholarly peers who lived off of government and land patrons. The chances of development oozed from the Northern Pakistani cities, little was left in the bustling cities to the south. Even though he was invited to the convention, his rejection to plan and build on such dangerous conditions earned his thanks and ultimately his dismissal. He was turned away as quickly as he was praised, and headed back to his hotel.

Mohammed never thought that arriving this late to a foreign home would be his solace for years of development. He stopped at the entrance and examined his reflection in the glass door. He reminded his family of his father, they had the same eyes that were beaten and wise. Mohammed's ability to dominate a room without being physically imposing matched his father's presence. His skin was lightly toasted from the days set examining the landscape of Islamabad. Unlike his father he was balding and his receding hairline paralleled his age.

He arrived late to the Pearl Continental in which he called home for the last five weeks. He loosened his tie as he entered the large Mediterranean inspired double glass doors. He walked past the check in counter and was greeted by two young receptionists.

One of them did a double take and leaned over to the other; they both blushed and laughed to themselves. The manager quickly emerged from the back room in which he had been eagerly waiting to deliver a message to Mohammed before retiring for the evening.

"Mr. Ahmed, I'm sorry to bother you sir but this message arrived while you were out."

"Thank you." He looked at the letter that was handed to him and immediately knew whom it had come from. "Hopefully she did not keep you on the phone for too long."

"Not at all sir." He quickly proclaimed. "Good night sir."

Mohammed blushed as he looked at the letter, knowing the sweet, honest and pure words that it had been derived from. He began walking toward the stairs to get to his room.

As he walked past the old grandfather clock, the loud ticking briefly took his eyes from the letter. "Eleven thirty, she must already be sleeping." He said to himself. He reached the bottom of the sweeping staircase and looked up, but as he was about to scale the first step a brass voice stopped him.

"Mohammed, Mohammed Ahmed?"

Mohammed looked down to balance himself and then turned to see a burly man standing behind him. The strangers eyes were squinted, and his grin outlined by his yellowish teeth and outlandish beard. The man had already extended his hand, by the time Mohammed was fully about face. Being the courteous man that he was, without hesitation Mohammed extended both his hands to shake this mans one hand. It was custom that the proper greeting was instilled from the beginning.

"As Salamu Alaikum my friend" withdrawing his hand to his heart after the hand- shake, as his mother had explained to him, was the ultimate example of brotherhood.

"I'm sorry to bother you at this hour, but the matter in which I must speak to you is very important, may we please sit down for some tea."

Mohammed sighed than smiled as he put the letter into his jacket pocket. "Of course, please." He signaled as he waited for the man to lead.

"Thank you, Mohammed, thank you, the stories of your civility are severely understated."

They headed toward the dining hall, without a word being said. Mohammed could tell that the man was nervous, the way he kept looking back at Mohammed and smiling. His steps were short and quick. The pacing caused him to breath harder and faster. It bothered some people the way Mohammed would try to come to a conclusion about a person before speaking to them. Mohammed, on the other hand, was used to being examined by people, whether it was his stature, demeanor, or overall handsome appearance, he could never really tell. Crossing through the elongated hall with a mirrored ceiling, Mohammed studied the architecture of the newly built building; it was something he knew, something he desired to know. Structures and blueprints were his Quran, and deciphering and planning through them was his purpose in life. He often compared himself to the materials he used as did his wife. "Your mind is like metal and heart like sand," She would always joke.

"The tea here is the best in city." The stranger slyly commented.

They finally made it through the hall to the dining hall and arrived to be greeted by massive crystal chandeliers, and perfectly aligned tables. The decorations were tacky but suited the design of the hall very well. A sea of red embroidered carpet balanced the thin line between modest and extravagant. There was a small stage in the center of the hall, no doubt used for all the wedding celebrations that took place here. The hall was dimmed and one host remained seated at a table staring at his pocket watch. He had a newspaper that was ruffled and spread across the set plates, napkins and silverware.

"May we sit, my friend?' The host immediately jumped up and looked around.

"Please, sit." Starting for the menu.

"No my friend, just tea." Mohammed stood and waited for his eager guest to be seated. He unbuttoned his suit jacket and took a seat as the waiter darted toward the kitchen. The room was darker than it had seemed outside and looking up at the chandelier only caused Mohammed unsteadiness. He crossed his legs and straightened himself out on the chair.

"Abass." The stranger almost shouted out. "My name is Abass."

"What is this concerning Abass?"

"I…Want to…I have to…" He could barely get the word out while chewing on his fingernails.

Mohammed scooted his chair closer to him and patted him on the leg to comfort him. "It's alright my friend, its late and we already have each others company so there is no need to be strictly formal."

"I'm sorry, will you excuse me please, I have to wash my hands before the tea arrives." He barked as he uncharacteristically and suddenly stood up.

"See formalities only cause discomfort. Go ahead, I and hopefully the tea will be waiting for you when you get back."

Abass nodded and swiftly made his way into the kitchen.

"Strange." Mohammed thought to himself. He quietly sat in the empty dining hall and picked the calluses on his hand. He opened his pocket watch, and gazed at the picture within. He remembered back to the time when the picture was taken, himself, his wife, Sophia, by his side and his first born daughter, Shehla, held within his arms. He noticed he was not carrying the pictures of his other children in his pocket, but knew that was the second thing he was going to look for, after calling his wife.

As seconds turned into minutes, he rechecked his watch and wondered if he should go in search of Abass. Before he made up his mind, the dining room doors opened and several men shuffled in toward the kitchen, carrying what looked like boxes of food and utensils. Mohammed smiled and nodded at anyone who paid him that same respect. They filed into the kitchen, one after another and opened the boxes to unload the contents. The host bustled out of the kitchen, with a large silver tray arranged with matching teacups and teakettle. He carefully set each piece of silverware on the table and whipped open a napkin and laid it upon Mohammed's lap.

"Sugar?"

"Two please, no milk."

The Host finished getting his tea and the table ready then retreated into the kitchen. Mohammed stirred his cup and set the spoon on the table, politely waiting for Abass to return. He continued to gaze at the decorations and check his watch, when suddenly a crashing noise was heard inside the kitchen. The door swung open just enough so that Mohammed could catch a glimpse of the mess on the floor. Potatoes were scattered all over the floor, the host walked with a hemp sack and recollected them one by one. Mohammed suddenly felt a cold wind down his spine, as he intently observed the man picking up the potatoes. His former life crept up inside him like a spider burrowing into his ear. He started to shiver and all the noises that were being made in the kitchen were slowly being tuned out. One by one the host gathered each potato and second by second Mohammed glimpsed into his own past. Second by second Mohammed was no longer in the Hotel.

2

India, 1937

Hyderabad was a fixture city on the old Silk Road that originated in Syria and died in the East. It was a hilltop city that had stunning views of the area surrounding the city. Much of the city was divided into blocks and within those were the housing districts divided by wealth and rank. The East Side of the Hyderabad was just built and a long narrowing road dissected the city in two. There were no street signs or names, you just had to know where you were going, or where you had been. Projects such as libraries and parks were being constructed upon the government and rich patrons requests. The Tariq housing district had originally been built for retired military personnel and rich British investors. Houses were set like prison columns and divided by cement walls three feet from each house. Flat rooftops and painfully similar housing structures resembled cement blocks, perfectly aligned, for as far as the eye could see.

A dirt lot, originally created to be a cricket field, swallowed the area in the midst of the homes. It was now being used to gather and burn the community trash of the Tariq housing district.

Mohammed's childhood home was directly in the course of the smoke that arose from the burnt refuge. His home was often empty, and other than the gardener and his parents servants, very quiet as well. Over the last few weeks friends, family, and most importantly, investors had invaded his home.

"Do you know what the difference is between you and I Mr. Ahmed? You believe that you could overcome any anything to get into god's graces, while I believe that I would overcome God himself to get through any anything. This world is changing and you have no part in its future, you are a ghost as it were. It takes a fool to know where another fool stands, so don't make the mistake of underestimating me." Ravinder Patel stood in the hallway of Ali Ahmed's home by side of his son Ehsan, his tall lanky frame was dominated by his sharp tongue and piercing wit. His son, though fragile in stature, had a beast of a heart and was willing to attack anything on his fathers command. Within Ravinder's frail hands were a plan and a legal land agreement that had already been signed by the Judge of the Hyderbad higher municipal court. Priceless paperwork meant to tear people from their homes, and uproot religious distinctions with integrated technology. Ravinder had tried handing the paperwork to Ali but Ali did not hesitate his hand in the offering. Ehsan, standing impatiently, grabbed the paperwork from his father and forced it into Ali's hands. Ravinder turned back to the door in which he was not allowed any further from and looked out past the gate. His son walked up next to him and turned back toward Ali and spit upon the floor. Ravinder looked at his son than Ali and just shrugged his shoulders; he began to make his way out. He noticed a quiet little boy positioned in the loft above the adjacent to the door. He turned back to Ali and signaled to the boy.

"You wouldn't want him to grow up in my world, would you?" He looked up and noticed the child throw a grimacing hand gesture his way.

"Mohammed! Your father should have taught you better than that, even though all he lives by is a myth. " He looked back at Ali. "Just look at the way I raised my son." He slapped Ehsan on the back and smiled. "You would be wise to teach your boy some manners, and it would be in your best interest to get those papers back to me as soon as you can. These matters don't need to take more than a few days to present themselves." He uttered as he stepped out the front door.

Ehsan stood and waited for Ali to flinch, from a physical standpoint Ehsan was no match for Ali. Ehsan looked up to the loft and gestured toward Mohammed. "You and your father are the same, you are both fucking idiots." He followed in his fathers footsteps and made for the front gate.

"See I told you, too nice of a house for a Sheik." Ravinder barked back toward his son. Ali stopped before closing the door and began to hesitate. He wanted to open the door and throw the paperwork back at Ravinder and then spit in Ehsan's face. He couldn't bring himself to do it, he could barely bring himself to lock the door. He finally closed the door and locked it, as the feeling of inevitable doom impended upon him. He felt weak in his knees and light headed, knowing that he had to face an audience of his peers.

Straightening himself up he looked down at the tiles that he had placed in entry room himself. The support posts that he had cast of steel and stone. The garden he laid with his bare hands and cool sweat. His future began to dawn upon him, as he knew his son would no longer carry on the tradition of this home. Looking up he was greeted by Mohammed cast down upon him, and carefree as the trials of this life were yet to meet him. After hearing a small ovation in his drawing room, he was brought back to his immediate reality. Ravinder's paper work still grasped in his hands, Mohammed's observance near the rooftop, and somewhere in between was Ali, left to present this material to his guests in the other room. He gathered himself, then dropped the paperwork on the floor. Stepping by the paper work he made his way to the drawing room and re-met with his guests who were patiently waiting for Ali to turn Ravinder and Ehsan away.

Ali entered a room full of inquiring faces, they had all stopped their conversations and waited for Ali to speak. "What do we do now, I suppose is the question on all of your minds?" He signaled to his servant to serve tea to all the guests. "Well let me tell you the best course of action is not to let this man encourage our violence. Our anger yes, but not our violence. Our mosques, temples, homes and businesses have been here and will be here far longer than anything he hopes to build."

"Ali," a soft voice from the back of the room commented. "He has the threatened to burn down the our temple, who's to say that he won't be the one burning our homes, or your mosque? He has already set fire to the farmers crops."

"It is all hearsay, to put blame solely on him for these crimes. Let us pray he is that dumb. We know that Judge Hamza has already signed off on the land development deeds that he wants, he cannot get anywhere without our agreement. He has the government's support but he needs ours."

"What is left? He has raised the prices on our produce, and the taxes he is able to charge are ridiculous, I say that the only way to end this strife is to give him the land and property he seeks so that the prices he controls will lower."

"Gentleman, understand that he will not stop until he gets what he believes to be his already. You and I have no sway over him or the Judge or the state of Hyderabad or even the police that he has bought. What we do have is the sway over each other and the majority of this land and its people. We have to stand together and stay united - it is the only way we ca-."

"I say that we ask the British for their assistance."

"The British only have a concern in what is good for their future! Ravinder is that future!" Ali shouted back.

"Perhaps we can raise our prices to match." A voice in the back of the room commented.

"You would only help deteriorate our community and cripple those who do not have the means that we do."

"What if we moved ourselves, to…say…Karachi.?" Those conflicting voices suddenly quieted down as an old man in the corner of the room became isolated from the larger group. The men sat down and looked at each other, in amazement and in agreement.

"Karachi?" The idea startled Ali, and at the same time raised his curiosity.

"Yes…you know that there is a large following of Muslims there already, I have been there and it seems that many Hindu's live there with them in relative peace. The numbers of Sikh's is few, that is true but if we were to travel together there is no reason to fear the unknown. I know that the idea of leaving your homes is unappealing but Karachi is bigger and more established than Hyderabad. The state and the police are not controlled by men but rather the people as a whole."

Many men sensed the room contemplating a change of scenery, "Karachi, but this is our home, we were raised here and many of our fore fathers died here."

"When will enough be enough?" The old man scoffed back. "Many of our homes already belong to Ravinder. Javed's house is burnt rubble. Do you know how the threats begin? With a head, Ali, a severed cows head. It greets you after a loud knocking on your door. There is no note, just a large head with empty eyes greeting your horrified children. If that is not enough then comes the beatings by the police. And what's more than that Ravinder gives the police free reign to break into our homes and rape our daughters and wives and kidnap our sons. His son Ehsan ruthlessly finds many of us in the streets and attacks us with no warning."

Ali stood dumbstruck as the thought of his wife under another man and his son bruised and battered crept into his mind. He began to hear her screams as she called out in pain for Ali to save her. His son stands, with one arm and two legs, on a street corner begging for money to satisfy his master's wealth. Even he understood that safety for his family was far and away. He would give every bone in his body for every smile and laugh that came from his wife and child; every happy moment within his life so that all tears would dry from the surface of their skin.

"It is true Ali," the old man's voice shattered Ali's subconscious. "That we all grew together and we wish that for our children as well. But we must have fairness in order for them to prosper and live on."

"Then you leave, I shall stay and fight." A Sikh man stood up and announced to his peers.

"You are a fool, a damn fool." The old man responded.

"You are all cowards for abandoning your homes."

Voices from around the room began to enter into the dispute. They pushed Ali back to the drawing room entrance door.

"Is it cowardice to protect your family!?"

"Only if I leave them in the hands of a coward like Ravinder."

"I would rather die than see my land in his hands."

"And I would rather die than see my family reduced to rags."

The voices in the room began to erupt, and Ali slipped back into his altered vision. The room slowed down and loud voices began to fall on deaf ears. The men within the room slowly began to stand and assert themselves upon one another. Ali walked out of his drawing room and into his study. He became so immersed in the thought of moving away that he didn't even notice Mohammed still in the loft staring down upon him. He walked into the dark room and turned on the light. A glimmer on the wall immediately caught his attention, it was his degree posted and neatly mounted on the wall. Like dead game it stared back at him "Osmania University class of 1922." That was ten years ago. He pulled the frame from the wall and stared at his reflection through it. Those ten years came so fast he thought to himself- his home; jobs and family were all non-existent at that point. "Awarded in Civil Engineering and Architecture" the words pierced his eyes and reminded him of all the words had led him to do. The road through the bazaar, the base of the town mosque and temple, the blueprints to the government buildings these were all created by these words. He held on and pulled the frame closer to himself. It felt warm, to warm from just hanging on the wall gathering dust. He felt a warmth centering from the back of the frame, it became warmer and warmer, then suddenly and without warning burst into a flame. Ali stood holding on to the flame and continued reflecting with it. The copper framework began melting into his hands; Ali refused to let go as the words within his degree began to blind him. His reflection turned into a viewing of bodies strewn upon the roadside and blood pouring on the curbside. His neighbors began begging on the streets, they stole and cheated among themselves. Though the one body lying on the street or face stealing from another was not of his wife's or his child's. He moved the frame like a pinball labyrinth looking for clues that they were alive, he raised his hands with the frame, then moved it closer to the light…Nothing. No faces. No smiles. No life. Anger consumed him, he raised the frame and began to fling it to the ground, and then a hand touched him on the shoulder. He was back in the drawing room with his guests, all of them looking to Ali for guidance. The hand tapped Ali again.

"It's time for Maghrib." An honest voice proclaimed.

Ali looked down and saw Mohammed waiting for a response.

"Abu, it is time for Maghrib. Will you lead the prayer?"

Ali sighed for a second, just enough to present Mohammed with his answer. Immediately Mohammed signaled to the servants to retrieve the rugs for prayer. The noise died down as the men assembled for prayer, and as quickly as the argument for fear upon the horizon emerged, it to had subsided.

Not a word was spoken at the dinner table that night. The only signs of life were the sounds of fresh naan being chewed with a mixture of vegetables and chicken curry. Ali's wife Noor sat across the table from Mohammed and next to Ali. Her red sari scarf covered half of her head, and the jingles from her bracelets sounded loudly as her skinny wrists could not hold them in place. Her lightly toasted skin illuminated her large hazel eyes and outlined the beauty that trimmed upon her lips. Ali often joked that if he was lost and looking for a path in the dark, Noor need do nothing but open her eyes. The only thing more captivating than her beauty was her inquiring mind. It was the reason Ali had gotten no peace at the dinner table that night.

Noor often looked to Ali for some sort of approval to talk about the preceding arguments that had taken place in their home. Every time Mohammed looked down at his plate to gather more food, Noor would quickly shoot Ali a look asking him to recognize the situation. He would respond by shaking his head and pointing to Mohammed, or looking at the clock. Noor knew that Mohammed was incredibly clever and it didn't matter when they talked about Ravinder.

"That is not going to just go away." She sat back in her chair and pointed to the paperwork lying on the floor. "This land is no longer ours or theirs." Pointing out the window, next door. "Ali you know tha-."

Ali slammed his hand down on the table and stared candidly at Noor. He did not remove his gaze until she lowered hers. Finally she gave in, trounced. Ali stood from the table and slammed his napkin into his bowl, He looked back at Mohammed to see that his gaze was fixed on his bowl, seeing no protest he made his way to the study.

The lights within the entry hall refined the study. Ali didn't bother turning on the light in the room, and hearing the loud generator come to life outside. Instead he withered inside and looked upon the small pictures spread amongst the blueprints and Quranic verses that lay upon Ali's massive study desk. He sat in his ripped leather chair and creaked it back and forth as he considered leaving his home.

"He is not afraid of any of those men, the only one he fears is you." The jingles from Noor's bell gave her away before her words did. "Why do you think he only comes to visit you, while sending the rest of the men letters and threats? It's because he fears you. He fears what you can become, and he fears the influence you have over the public. And even if his threats end, his son's will continue."

Ali scoured through pictures of Mohammed when he was an infant. His wedding pictures began to subsurface and in turn bury the blueprints of a library.

"Ali! Ali say som-."

The picture within Ali's hand framed the beginning of his adulthood. Bathed in flower wreaths, and pasted in red, they both looked unready, but they both seemed… calm.

"I can give up everything in this world, I can give it all up, everything except you and Ali."

Noor breathed a sigh of relief and walked closer toward Ali and the desk in the study. She lightly tugged the picture within Ali's hands and looked down to see herself in a red wedding gown "You won't have to give us up."

"Today that old man stood in my home and told me what had become of his wife and children. How could I let the same fate befall you and Mohammed?"

"I know that Ravinder is a scared, minute man with much money. It should take more than that to move you."

Ali creaked in his chair again and again, "As he was leaving today he called me a Sheik. Sheik… you and I know the only ones who call me Sheik are the servants. He has been here; he has his eye fixed on this block, and on this home… He is looking and he is planning to take our home and our lives." He looked out the door into the hallway without rising from his chair. "Our lives began here, but they will not end here it seems."

"What do you want to do than, if we cannot fight him, or resist him, then what will we do?"

"When the old man mentioned to everyone, about moving to Karachi, I have to admit it was not the first time I had pondered this myself." Ali removed a key from within his pocket and unlocked a drawer in his desk. " I was just surprised that I was not the only one who had thought about it." He pulled out a beige colored folder and reached into the right pocket and pulled out a thick packet of papers. He dropped it upon his desk and the sound resonated like a judge dropping his gavel.

Noor set the picture upon the edge of the table and picked up the packet and was immediately struck by the first words: "Land Rights Maleer, Karachi awarded to Ali Ahmed." She did not raise her head and felt paralyzed with relief.

"These rights were granted to us by our family who already reside in Karachi. They have plans to secure our land, it is already built and ready, all the state needs is our word to transfer."

"Our friends, our family, they are all here."

"So is Ravinder and Ehsan beyond them. Their fate will be the same as mine if we were to stay. I want to stay, I built this house with my bare hands, but I cannot attach myself to the past anymore."

"I don't care what happens as long as we are safe. You, Mohmmed and I. If you go, Mohammed and I will follow you to no end."

"If we leave we forfeit all we have to Ravinder. It is difficult to leave, he is constantly watching. If we were to leave it would raise suspicion and doubt among our neighbors."

"Ali, at this point all that stands between him and Hyderabad are your sites and this block. I know it, this whole block knows it; they came here to size each other up, to see whom would be the first to indulge. Money has a tighter bond than loyalty these days."

"I have spent my whole life here Noor. From my first step until this very moment, Hyderabad is as much my family as you and Mohammed. I cannot bare to see our past and futures destroyed to develop something foreign. But we are indeed fragile and will probably have to give everything in order to resurrect in another city."

"When you say it like that Karachi doesn't seem that far away." Noor replied sarcastically.

A thunderous pounding on the front door resounded throughout the house. Ali and Noor caught a quick glimpse of Mohammed as he ran to answer the door. They heard the one side of the entry double door open and stunned by the cry that followed.

"Abu!"

Ali ran out of the study toward the scream, but he could not see what Mohammed was screaming about. As he quickly approached the door the abhorrent scene became apparent. Lying, bleeding and staring empty up at Ali was a severed cows head, the blood that streamed out ran a trail to the gate that compounded the home. It grinned up at them with its open eyes, and pressed them back with the surrounding flies. The puddle of blood reached the entry stair into their home, and the shadow it cast upon the tiles was that of a red sea. Its tongue protruded from the cut upon its right cheek, and the yellowish teeth grinded into the strings of fat that held the mouth shut. Noor ran to the door and covered

Mohammed's eyes as she yelled aloud to the servants to come and clean the mess. She looked up to Ali and they both silently acknowledged the symbol upon their doorstep.

Ali stepped outside his home and into the courtyard adjacent to the entry gate. An empty home across the dirt refuge lot was set ablaze. Neighbors had gathered from their homes and into the intersecting streets. Ali signaled for Noor to take Mohammed back into the house. He exited his property and saw his neighbor Maaz out upon the street as well. Ali raised his hand to signal Maaz over to him: "Did you see who did this?"

"Ali, there have been so many men moving quietly throughout the compound, I don't know who is a resident and who isn't."

Ali signaled for to Maaz to follow him. Upon entry into the gate Maaz stopped dead in his tracks when the scene of the blood pool greeted him. Ali continued into the house and secured two large plastic drums. On the way back into the courtyard he had to physically withdraw Maaz from the dead sight to get him to follow him to the well outside the homes and near the centered dirt lot. They reached the well outside the home and filled both drums with water and ran to the emblazoned home.

Other neighbors and a modest fire patrol met them. Quickly forming into an assembly line that stretched from the well, they focused their attention upon the fire. The smoke reached the skyline and to the point of recognition for the whole city. Support posts began to snap, with the intense heat battling back at the group of ant-like workers. The steel melted like wax and the roof collapsed to the floor to blow out the bottom floor windows. Men moved from the wells toward the home, upon the way dropping the drums of water. The useless effort had subsided as everyone discontinued the heroism. Silence infected the mass, and struck them with a cold stone touch. Fire engulfed the home, and became the lullaby that rested the pillars to ash. The orange glow upon the faces and the homes died and returned the land to darkness. Ali dropped the buckets within his hands and was the first to retire from the large group. His walking turned to jogging and jogging to running. He paced toward his home, toward his family.

As he made it back to the housing compound he noticed the gate lock had been cut, and footsteps had been outlined in the blood. The servants were upon the entry tiles cleaning up the blood. He walked up to the head and picked it from the floor. It bled upon his kurta and on to his sandals. He turned back to the servant that had just turned the corner and asked him for the papers that lay on the entry floor. The servant ran to the door removed his sandals entered the home and retrieved the papers for Ali. Upon handing him the papers the servant reached to take the head from Ali's hands. Instead Ali jawed open the heads teeth and inserted the papers then clamped the mouth shut. He went to the gate and opened it to the deserted street. He placed it along with the papers in its mouth upon the gravel outside the gate. He noticed the footsteps imprinted within the blood were his own, the lock that was cut, however, was not by his doing.

Ali rushed back into his home and began to check all the windows and doors leading in. There was no way that anyone made it past the servants positioned at the front door. Ali checked the loft closet, kitchen pantry, and the drawing room hold. His search for an obstruction became a search for his family. He looked in the master bedroom for any signs of disruption. The closet light was turned on and a shadow was moving back and forth. He opened the sliding door to witness Noor struggling to get Ali's hunting rifle down from one of the shelves. Mohammed was crouched in the corner behind two coats. Ali ran to her aid and took the handle and signaled to her to go to Mohammed. With gun in hand he locked the master bedroom door and barricaded himself along with his family in the closet. The hall light was the only light that Ali would allow into the closet, he feared that anything that could give his family away would give his family away.

The light in the hall started to fade as the generator began to weaken. The only sign of life throughout the house was now Ali's rampant heart thumping to the tense beat of survival.

Morning would bring no comfort, as the clouds amongst the sky shadowed the mood among the eve. Ali had not dared close his eyes. He had dared not remove himself from the company of his family. Light crept into the closet, and onto the face of Noor, who lied sleeping and protecting Mohammed. Ali opened the closet door and cast himself into the bedroom, gun cocked and drawn. There was no sign of disturbance other than the one Ali made creating a barrier to the closet.

The rest of the house was alive and bustling, keeping up with its normal routine. Breakfast was on the table, the floors were swept, the laundry was drying and the gate-keeper was about tending to the broken lock.

"Good Morning Sahib." The voice of the servant nearly caused the gun to go off.

"Abdullah!... is everything in shape?" his voice wavered.

"Of course Sahib. The lock is fixed and that head is gone. We kept a lookout for you Sahib. You are our family too Sahib."

Abdullah was a servant to Ali for over 12 years now. He was from the Punjab state, his darker appearance and bare-feet-wherever attitude usually defined his lower caste status. Ali didn't believe him to be a friend or confidant, but rather a member of his service. For the past year now Abdullah's behavior has been more protective toward Ali's family, he always asks to accompany Noor and Mohammed if they were to leave alone on an errand. There was nothing unusual about Abdullah's motif, rather his demeanor grew with time and patience. He often played with Mohammed and was the head of the service for the household. Ali's trust in him came from his years of service and ability to be humble and honest.

"Yes…Well, here. Give this to the others as well." He handed Abdullah one hundred rupees. "Now please, go and prepare our luggage."

"Yes sahib. Where will you be going?"

Ali gave Abdullah a piercing stare. "Wherever I please!"

"No disrespect sahib, I was just looking out for your well being."

"My comfort comes with my patience, the little I have left will not be spent upon someone of your class! Go now!"

"Right away sahib." Abdullah pocketed the money and went out the servant entrance into the alley between the house and the cemented wall.

Ali checked the rest of the house and made sure nothing was unaccounted for:s "They are after us, not our things or the servants" he thought to himself. He went back to the kitchen and sat at the table and placed the gun upon the floor next to his feet. He called aloud to Noor and Mohammed before indulging and was halfway through his meal by the time they came down to eat. Mohammed was just awakening, and Noor joined him in exhaustion and fatigue. They came down, and were greeted by a new Ali, an eager one, and a scared one.

Before they were able to sit the sound of a car pulling up to the gate could be heard in the distance. Doors opened and slammed shut, feet shuffled and an iron echo rang at the front gate. Ali laid his gun on his chair as he stood up. He indicated to Noor to hide her and Mohammed. Opening the front door he could see the tops of soldiers heads and the roof of a military vehicle. He winced, then calmly opened the front door and walked casually to the front gate.

"What is your business?" Ali barked. He looked at the shadows on the ground and saw a filed line of men created. "State your business!"

"Ali open this gate right now!" The voice was familiar to him; he knew that Ravinder would send a worthy henchman, but not his best.

"Ehsan!? It seems your fathers will is greater than his concern."

"Open this gate, you stubborn ass!"

Ali opened the door and was immediately overwhelmed by the soldiers stomping into his housing compound. Ehsan casually strolled in behind them and closed the door behind him. He looked at the entrance to the home and saw that Noor and Mohammed were standing witness.

"Your servants have done an excellent job re-securing your home. It's so clean you wouldn't believe that there was once blood upon these white tiles. We must remedy that…again."

Ehsan strolled closer to the house and back toward Ali, looking at the ground checking the framework on the house. He studied the strength of the support beams and the pattern of the archway at the entry door. With his hands locked behind his back he walked back to Ali and laughed to himself as he made his way to the garden upon the gated boundary. The petals upon the flowers were as soft as the fresh soil he walked upon; the scent was as crisp as cool mornings he imagined within this house. He picked the largest one in bloom and ran the orange petals across his palm. He went back to the group of soldiers and whispered something to the captain. The captain looked at Noor, grinned and nodded back to Ehsan.

"Sheik, sheik, sheik. Your home is indeed wonderful. It's a shame someone would want to sully its beauty. Do you know the name of this flower?"

Ali stood and gave no reply.

"Well I don't. It's amazing how we know so little about such beautiful things, or what it takes to make them. A flower is no different from a person, a home or a city. It takes time to develop; it takes caution and extreme patience to create something so precious and vulnerable. You care for it and nurture it as if it blood were running in your veins." He put the flower into both of his hands and then squeezed as hard a he could, he opened his hand and it fell to the ground crumbled and destroyed. The petals had crease marks upon them and the stem was bleeding a clear substance. It laid on the ground and was crippled, and battered begging Ali to pick it up. "Things that are that defenseless as so... feeble. They are created to die just like everything else in this damn city." He reached into his coat pocket and pulled a white and red stained envelope from it.

"Why were these on the floor?" He had the dried bloodstained papers within his elongated fingers. "More importantly why are they not signed?"

Ali just stared at Ehsan with a blank face, encouraging his anger-induced response, instead Ehsan laughed and signaled to his men to gather around.

"Go check the rubble of the burnt house, there has to be scrap metal, and steel pieces about."

The soldiers looked upon one another confused, than assembled and marched out the front gate. Back inside the home Ehsan waited for the thunderous march to reach a suitable distance. He started to loosen his shirt at the neck and around his wrists.

"My father seems to fear you, but I don't." He crumpled the papers in his hands and formed it into a ball. "We'll have your cooperation one way or another!" He threw the papers upon Ali's face and began to bull rush him.

"Ali!" Noor yelled out to try to make Ali catch Ehsan.

At first Ali looked back at Noor but then was overwhelmed by the force that had taken him to the ground. He was stunned by the turn of events, but his mood quickly changed when Ehsan was on top of him fist pounding into his rib cage. Ehsan quickly threw punches as he positioned himself atop Ali. His pointy joints provided him with an extra weapon to use against his opponents. He could feel elbows stabbing at his stomach, and knees hammering at his thighs. Ali used his strength to throw Ehsan back and stop most of his barrage. Ali got to his knees as Ehasn struggled to get to his feet. Again he bull rushed Ali and instead of being caught by surprise Ali unleashed his fist upon Ehsan's throat. Choking, Ehsan fell upon his backside and coughed twice, more than enough time for Ali to begin his assault. He stomped on Ehsan's chest and laid two sharp kicks upon the side of his face. Ehsan grabbed Ali's left foot and wrestled him to the ground once again asserting his dominance upon him. This time he managed to weasel his arm around Ali's neck. The pressure began to surmount, his eyes grew red, his face pink, and his will subsiding. A loud smack was heard like a cricket bat hitting a ball, the pressure eased and Ehsan slumped over and fell to the ground. Ali gasping for air looked beside him to see, a familiar yet unwanted sight standing near. He recognized the size and shape of those feet, short limbs, and uneasy look. To his dismay it was Mohammed grasping onto Ali's gun. The butt of the gun was facing out and had shards of hair and blood falling from it. Mohammed was standing still, and the force used to create such a hit seemed uncharacteristic, even for anyone of Ali's relation.

Ali looked upon the silent Ehsan and noticed the large gash among the left side of his skull. Ehsan was still breathing, but the heavy panting of Mohammed took over the entire scene.

Noor remained at the entrance upon the stairs. She did not hesitate or come to the aid of her family. Her hand covered her mouth and her mood escalated from fear, to concern to survival. She did not jump to help her husband; she doomed her son to conceive her fate. She watched as Ali lie on the floor and Mohammed stand above him, savior and condemner. She should of jumped to help or at least call for help, but all the evils that conspired within Ehsan held her in place.

Mohammed was trembling while holding the gun in his hands. His face was pale and his eyes remained fixed on the capsized Ehsan. He went to raise the gun to the air once again but slowly brought in down by his side. He did not smile, he did not say a word, and instead he looked at his father who was gasping to recover his breath. Mohammed was always a quiet boy but not violent. His fist remained clenched to the gun, his heart pounding and knees trembling. He reached over to his father and offered his hand to help him up. What was done was done, and as quickly as Mohammed had struck that blow he had bid farewell to his adolescence.

Ali managed to his feet and grabbed Mohammed and the gun and ran inside. He ran past Noor who remained still and screamed for her to quickly follow. Abdullah appeared near the staircase with suitcases in hand.

"Are you ready to go sahib?" Abdullah remarked, unusually unaware of what just conspired.

"Get the car ready now!"

Noor who had just come from retrieving precious heirlooms followed Abdullah. Ali beckoned for Abdullah to get the car ready and meet them out in near the gate. He grabbed Noor by the hand while still carrying

Mohammed in his other arm. He headed to the study and retrieved blueprints and land deeds. He quickly set Mohammed down in the chair outside the study. He had one important thing to retrieve and could not leave without it. It was in his safe behind the stacks of books that he holds his last resort. Mohammed quickly opened the vault and scurried through papers money and jewelry. He pocketed most of the money but was looking for something else. Then a glimmer of light shined into the dark crevasse and exposed the instrument he desired. He slowly pulled it out and examined it in the light. Putting it in his coat pocket he thought to himself 'this is a last resort.' He paused and felt the elongated metal pressed against his chest.

He quickly gathered himself and his family that was waiting out near the study. They ran out to the car that stood idling next to an unconscious Ehsan. Ali, fearing the soldiers acknowledging the car, nearly threw Mohammed and Noor in the back and shut the door.

Abdullah looked on from the drivers seat. "Sahib, this does not bode well for you."

"Just drive! Back out slowly and take us to the edge of the city. Take us to my library." Ali got into the front seat and tried to breath easier. He signaled for Abdullah to back out of the gate. Ali watched his house gradually slip away from him. The gate was still open and the reflection of the sun brightened the home to a blinding sight. The bricks he laid by himself, the flowers that lay within the garden, it was all lost. No longer afraid for himself he was fleeing for his family's life. He would've stayed; he would've fought all the soldiers he would've died for his home. His home was a shadow among the trail of dust, the uncertain void that swallowed his home was now pushing his family to the edge of the city.

They had safely driven out of the Tariq housing district without being noticed by the soldiers. Upon the way Ali went through the actions of what just happened in his head again and again. The consequences kept presenting themselves; he no longer cared for his home or his wealth, only his family. Several minutes later the car arrived at the large newly built library. The windows reflected the light of the sun onto the near by buildings. It was placed upon the edge of the city and was the last civilized building until the next city many, many miles away. Yet instead of getting out to run, they just sat and waited, and waited, and waited.

They sat as the car struggled to stay alive, Ali stared through the glass at the library he had built, he knew it was no longer his, was no longer going to stand along with many of his other creations. He looked down at the blueprints in his hands and the red paper work upon his lap.

Abdullah began to jostle in his seat. "What now sahib? Shall I take you further?"

"I have to end this, I have to make this right." His words shattered the silence of several hours.

"This will never end, this will not stop until he has what he wants." He looked back at Noor and Mohammed. "I have to go see him."

"Ali jaan, no. We must go together, let us leave this place."

"To where? He will constantly hunt us, no longer does he just want land; he wants blood. He will want vengeance... or these." He held up the land deeds in his hands. "He will be after you and Mohammed. I have to go see him and give him all of this. The blueprints, the land, the deeds, it is all his."

"He will kill us if we go."

"If I don't go he will kill all of us! You are not coming with me; I cannot risk you coming with me. By now he has already dispatched his people to look for Mohammed. He will want vengeance, the same vengeance performed upon his son."

"We will not go anywhere without you."

"You will go where you are told! Please Noor hear me. If they catch Mohammed they will slit his throat and not care how it reads in the paper. I must go now and beg for his life. You must flee with Mohammed and meet me in the village."

"How do we even know Ehsan is dead?"

"It doesn't matter. What was performed upon Ehsan he will surely impose upon Mohammed if he gets the chance."

They got out of the car and opened the trunk of the car to find something to disguise Noor with. They opened her suitcases and pulled out a burqa, she slid into it, and it covered her from head to toe only to expose her eyes. Ali embraced both Mohammed and Noor and began to bid them farewell. He knew the journey he set before Noor would test her beyond her recognition.

"Two days… meet me by the bridge on the west side of the river."

Abdullah stepped out from the driver side of the car. "Ali Sahib, allow me to accompany them."

"No you must come with me, and you must not speak a word to the others of where Noor is headed."

"Please sahib, I will protect them, they are my family as well… Let me help them."

"You will come with me, and say nothing!"

Abdullah bowed his head and sat back in the car.

"Wait Ali, what of Mohammed, how are we going to hide him?" said Noor.

Mohammed looked in the trunk, removed the luggage, spare tire, then finally something presented itself. A large brown sack, it was full of potatoes. Ali emptied a portion of it, reached agreement with Noor of Mohammed's disguise then turned to Mohammed. Noor held one side while Ali grasped the other. They both looked at Mohammed who was getting one last look at Hyderabad.

3

Ali had Abdullah pull the car out of the library entrance. The car was quiet and still alive after staying idle for so long. It took nearly an hour for Noor and Mohammed to disappear from Ali's sight. Abdullah said nothing and the ride to Ravinder's house became a pilgrimage within Ali's mind. Ali didn't know what he was going to say or how he was going to say it. All he knew was that Ravinder would gain nothing from his death, but the bargain for his family was much more of a challenge. The thought of forgiveness on Ravinder's part did not seem logical at this point. He knew that he had to deal with this like he would any other business transaction- swiftly and diligently. This was different though, how would he present his son as a fact or figure. Would his actions cause Ravinder to give a counter offer? His only option was to go and present an offer that gives him and his family leverage.

The drive to Ravinder's house was one Ali had taken many times before. Although he had never been within its gates, he was perfectly aware of its location. His house was perched atop the tallest hill in Hyderabad. It gave him a distinct view of all the land and… his enemies. The massive gate they rolled up to was twice the size of Ali's. When they approached the gatekeeper emerged from his shack on the side of the cemented wall. He approached the car and peered in. Upon immediate recognition of Ali he sprinted to the gate and unlocked it. It was almost as if he was being expected. He looked at Abdullah, but he just shrugged and looked on. The sharp sound of molded iron resonated as one side of the gate swung open to invite the car through. From there the drive to Ravinder's home seemed like an eternity. The house itself did not become evident until the car rounded a patch of forestry. Bright lights were cast upon gray statues in enormous fountains. His four-story home was more like a government building than an abode. Seven beautiful cars lay outside the sweeping staircase that entered into the home. Each of the twelve windows facing Ali gave view into a different room- dining, luxury, library, and recreation. His home was an oasis among the shrewd mounds that Ali called home. Ali and Abdullah both got out of the car but Ali motioned for Abdullah to stay abound. He walked up the stairs with all his life's work within his hands. Each step became more embellishing than the next. He walked up to the door and was immediately and shockingly greeted by Ravinder. He stood there and looked upon Ali, his hands clinched and unclenched again and again. Before Ali could say anything Ravinder broke the uneasy peace.

"Your God works in mysterious ways." He smirked while sizing Ali up from head to toe. "My son lay wounded in his bed and the reason stands defenseless at my door. Perhaps a gift… or an offering?"

"Your sons reasons for pain come by his own hand. He should know better. Like you said, you would be wise to teach your son some manners."

Ravinder pulled a cigar from his coat pocket but didn't bother to light it. "God does work in mysterious ways."

"I am here to negotiate."

"You are here because your family flea's away, and blood rights need to be settled."

"You are not out for blood!"

"I am out for whatever will give me restitution… Perhaps it is not your blood, but an offering of some sort."

"I am here to do business. I know we have caused each other much harm, It should not, however, stand between us as businessmen."

"You know, if you were anyone else your family would be dead right now. But not you…old friend."

Ali smiled knowing that Ravinder was weak to his game. "Blood is not a leverage, but perhaps these are. Even you can get nothing without my say so." He held up the paperwork.

Ravinder looked at the work and stood silent. He peered past Ali and down to the car he came in.

"They will only be yours if you promise my families life."

"What if I just take them from your dead hands."

"You can, but you cannot claim rightful ownership, even the British have strict laws of these legalities. You will need the all the original paperwork granted by this Government, one that I have in the car with my servant."

"It's a shame…all that you built will be smashed to the ground, anything with 'Ali Ahmed' shall be burnt to the ground and given commercial rights. Your family shall be as quickly forgotten as they were remembered. You will be an after thought, a whisper. And all this just for their lives."

Ali knew he would cross this compromise inevitably; the thought of his life's work would be dismantled. He no longer would carry any sway within Hyderabad, he would be known as a deserter, a coward. Would it work, could he get away with it? He wanted thought of this plan for longer than he knew but it still had its complications. Would he be able to get out of the city? His only hope was to try and hope Ravinder took what he offered. None of this seemed to deter his resolve in saving his family. He knew that Ravinder would cast the first stone on his family if given the chance. He was torn between his career and his family. He had spent most of his life on both and many times seemed to care for both equally. He nurtured and grew with both, but knew that any life beyond his was astringently appealing. He hoped his son had a developing knowledge and interest in Architecture. He reached into the chasm of his mind and retrieved the memories of Mohammed, and the life he wanted to see beyond his.

"Yes…you may have it all, I will give you access to what you require but I must have word that you will not harm them."

"Agreed." Ravinder calmly smirked. "Now hand them over."

"Here. All you require is in this envelope…" Ali felt his stomach deepen and his head spin.

Ravinder grabbed hold of his final puzzle piece. "How very simple."

Ali did not extend his hand in any offering; instead he bowed his head slightly in agreement.

"What of the other paperwork?" Ravinder questioned.

"I'll retrieve those for you."

"That won't be necessary." As he turned to leave he noticed Ravinder signal to Abdullah who was still waiting in the car. Abdullah rose out of the car and began walking to the two men. Ali was confused and shouted at Abdullah to stay his ground.

"Abdullah. Do not approach!"

Abdullah came up to Ali and glanced at him than looked at Ravinder and shook his hand. Than he smirked at Ali and took out a large thick envelope and handed to Ravinder.

"They are headed East."

Ali was baffled, the shock left him pinned to his stance.

"Abdullah you dog. You motherless dog." Ali yelled as he constrained himself from attacking.

Ravinder calmly smiled, "It's interesting how money can dissolve allegiance."

"Abdullah you are my servant. After all the years I cared for you in my home."

"Sahib, I care for your family I really do. But I care for mine much more."

Ravinder handed Abdullah a wad of cash, it was bundled neatly and thickly.

"What of our accord?" Mohammed beckoned.

"It is true that I promised not to harm you're family, but how can I deter the men I have already sent out to do so?"

Ali still did not see all the signs of Abdullah's back slinging and like a flash of light it became clear to him. He packed his bags; he had the key to the gate. Sadly he was closer to Ali than any man ever was.

"Now. If there is anything else, leave. It would be wise for you to leave right away. Leave your home. Leave the goodbyes… Just leave."

Abdullah took the keys to the car out of his pocket and handed them to Ali. He looked upon him as a dog would a master, begging to be petted. Ali did not shake his hand or give him words of encouragement he didn't even look him in the eye. He just took the keys and headed toward the car. He thought about his last option, but it was the option of a desperate man, and he had indeed become desperate. On his way down he stopped and stood for a few seconds. He reached within his coat pocket and began to feel for he sharp instrument he had concealed. It began to call his name, as it begged for Ali to use it. Ali had only ever used it once, and had swore from that point on never to use it again in vain. He felt down the leather grasp to the sharp edge. He slowly pulled it from his coat pocket and held the instrument with both hands. 'Now is the time, old alliances cannot be repaired.' The horror of what Ali was about to propose was tugging at the angel upon his left shoulder. He thought as he turned back to Abdullah and Ravinder, about how Ravinder had perfectly set up this very moment, unmoving to Ali and unknowing to Abdullah. He concealed the instrument behind his back and made his way back up the stairs directly to his enemy.

Abdullah and Ravinder stood still and were not moved by Ali's return to them. His demeanor had changed and he was walking up with some different intent.

"It is a good thing that you brought Abdullah. I should have seen all the signs before. Ravinder, we are as clever as we are cruel."Ali said as he stopped a few feet away from Ravinder. 'Blood Rights must be paid' he said to himself. Ravinder and Ali both looked upon the unknowing Abdullah. Ali reached for his shoulder "You should have never brought yourself into this."

4

Winds in the distance brought life to the empty and barren lands that were once a fertile farmland. Purple skies were illuminating the fires that had been set to clarify homes and crops. The harsh dry season had turned the Indian countryside into the sea of blowing dirt. Hyderabad was a shadow in the distance, and looked like a beacon of rest for eastbound travelers. The hard land slowly began to turn into mud as the river that divided the land provided nutrition for the dying wayside. Hyderabad must have been an oasis, to be created out of such conditions. A village on the Westside of the river provided a sanctuary for the fleeing Noor and her hidden accomplice.

Dusk was quickly approaching and Noor knew she had to get to the other side of the river before night fell. She was moving as quickly as she could and could hear her captors coming up quickly behind. Her sandals provided her with no support in the mud as each step she took sunk her deeper and deeper. Each step became more taxing and the sack she bore over shoulder was now cutting into her skin. With each strengthened step came a weakened heart. She could feel Mohammed twisted and crumpled against her back.

From within the brown sack she could hear Mohammed's breathing become a choir. His body became a medium for bruising by the potatoes crushed against him. It had been dark since they had set out days ago. He could not feel his legs and the crouched fetal position he was placed in began to feel normal. His right arm wrapped around his back, while his left leg met his chin.

"Amma, please let me out, I cannot see I cannot breath…I don't feel…anything."

His words stabbed at Noor's heart, she wanted to stop and let him out. "Be still Mohammed, I will find a place for us to rest."

She saw a light glimmer inside what appeared to be an abandoned farmhouse in the distance. Knowing full well that there was no way that she could make it beyond the river by nightfall she weighed the consequences between heading to the river or toward the faded light. She heard men with coarse voices disperse as if to cover more ground. She now knew the farmhouse was her only choice. When she arrived at the door she could see the roof had been torn off and that wooden planks solidified the broken windows. Lightly rapping on the door she didn't want to give cause for her captors to find her. The door creaked open and a voice emerged from the dark.

"State your purpose."

" Let me in, please help me." She begged

"There is no place for you in here."

"You have to help me, please, just until the morning."

"Sister, there is no place for you in here, go to the village."

"My feet will not carry me that far, I am in need for a place to rest."

The door creaked as if to close, but stayed slightly open. Noor heard whispers in the background and could make out three different people.

"There is no place in here, but there is a small hidden cellar behind the house, go there and stay hidden."

It seemed odd to Noor that the voice was so put off, and that such a place was hospitable for people to live and survive. Her hesitation was sidetracked for the comfort of her cargo. The door closed and Noor immediately made for the side of the house. She felt her away across the house and stepped lightly with her feet to identify the cellar door. When she passed the second window the floor beneath her became hollow and unstable, she reached down and searched for some sort of latch. Although the she could sense some sort of opening, the dead leaves, dried dirt, and loose silt had covered it. The men's voices were getting heavier, as were their footsteps, they knew someone was out here and the hungered to find some poor soul. The patting to find the latch turned to digging as Noor was now clawing to search for a latch. She saw a torch light up and outline the sides of the house and a deep voice shouted to the others. She could feel the omnipresence collapsing around her, she did not dare stop, and she did not dare look up. Her fingers reached the latch and began struggling to pull out the O shaped handle. At last she had found it, and pulled so gently, enough so that an opening barely allowed her and the sack to fit through. As she entered the underground shelter, her hands became her eyes and feet, feeling each step until she reached the floor. The door closed above her and the small dark damp room became clearer and clearer to her adjusting eyes. Removing the sack from her shoulder, Noor felt the fresh tear in her shoulder rescind to the middle part of her back. She could barely sit up straight and had to adjust her posture so her head did not hit the cellar ceiling. When the sound of footsteps began dissipating, Noor began to untie the sack and carefully removing the potatoes within. Slowly the top of a head began to appear in the middle of the sack.

"Mohammed, Mohammed its okay for now. Come out."

The head turned into a face, and the face into body, until a small boy emerged from the burlap. He rubbed his eyes as it to adjust them to the light. Mohammed moved around and stretched his tiny body that had been surrounded and pressured by potatoes.

"Are you alright Mohammed?" she asked while holding the sides of his arms, she went to touch his face. "How you look like your father." She sighed. "Inshallah we will see him soon, he is waiting for us."

Mohammed looked around the cramped hole and tried to make out patterns in the wall. It reminded him of his servant's quarters in Hyderabad, how small they were and how the size of his room encompassed his servant's entire house. He remembered the way the servants would come out and play cricket with him, then retire to tend to the home chores. He thought they were brothers or at the very least related because they all lived on the same compound. Now that they fled without them he knew that was a farce and that his family thought very differently about them. "Why did we have to leave?"

Noor looked down and back at her child, shocked she replied, "Because we're going to join your father."

"Why did we not bring Abdullah?"

"His place is back in Hyderabad, ours is in Karachi."

"But he lived with us, why can he not live with us here?"

Noor knew that there was no way to get around the subject with her inquiring child. It was a sore matter and one that she knew would touch on the fact of their fleeing. Noor always knew that there was an intense pressure between religious officials and modern bureaucrats in Hyderabad. Ravinder was a profound businessman that had moved himself and his businesses into the area years earlier. Through the help of his colleagues he was able to cleanse the area of any religious believers and officials including Muslims, Hindus, and Sikhs- he was Hyderabad's Nero.

"Abdullah does not belong with us, it is only you, I, and your father."

Mohammed paused and reversed his thoughts. He was still holding his father's gun in his hand and Ehsan was still face down on the ground. He knew what he had done crippled his family's future, but he didn't know it would mean running for their lives. He wondered if the last of his father he saw was through a burlap sack. He knew he would no longer play with Abdullah in the street or the neighbors across the lot.

"What is Karachi like?"

Noor had only been there once, the sounds, the smell, the amount of people- it had all probably gotten bigger by that point.

"It's big, very, very big. And more of your aunts, uncles, and cousins are there."

"Will we have a home?"

"Yes jaan."

"Will it be as big? Will I have my own room again?"

"We will see jaan…Let's try and get some sleep now, okay."

She laid a sheet down over some hay she found in the corner of the cellar. Mohammed stretched himself out upon the make-shift bed. Noor put her head next to Mohammed's and shut her eyes; at least when she did that the room was a little brighter. She was faced with the reality of living a life without Ali, and possibly without Mohammed. The past turned to present, and all promises within a new life began to fade. An eternal void greeted Noor like the darkness she laid within. An uncertain future was beckoning at her heart, and an unknown assurance dried up any hope of a peaceful life. These feelings were foreign to her and for the first time in her life she felt helpless, and alone. The first journey she had ever made came at the mid point in her life. It was wasted upon her age, and shrilled against her desire. The only comfort she had was knowing that she would wake next to her son, and the prospect of being with her beloved.

The night came as a whisper, as the winds died down and gave way to a symphony of silence. Noor did not dare sleep as she waited for the morning light to pierce through the cracks in the cellar door. It had been a long time since she last heard the beat of her pursuers trails. Dawn was but a few minutes away and in the distant village the call to Morning Prayer had begun to echo.

Noor grew anxious and weary, the tight cramped space became suffocating and with every ray of light- smaller. She had to open the door and once again look onto her new journey. The thought of her captors waiting outside the cellar brought about second judgments. The news of something terrible happening to Mohammed yielded her advance. But the promise she made to her husband brought her to her knees, and the thought of seeing him again gave her the courage to swing open the door. It was heavier than she had remembered, and the thud it created was outlined in the dust cloud plumed over her.

Mohammed woke from his slumber and saw his mother move out of the cellar and onto the deserted farmland. The cellar seemed smaller with the light casted into it, and much less musty. It was a strange time for him. It was one of the first times he could remember being truly alone with his mother. It brought him more angst than it did comfort, for after all it was her duty to protect him from harm. A duty Mohammed knew she was incapable of. Mohammed followed his mother out of the cellar, the sunlight struck down and the wind had ceased. There was something unusual in the landscape; to one side of the river there was a bounty of green shrubbery and vast blue sky, the other side, the side they were on seemed... dead. Noor peered into the window of the house but it was completely abandoned. Odd, she did not hear anyone leave, or even make a sound. There were no footprints, there was nothing left from anyone, it was as if no one had been in the house or out following them. Mohammed looked around to see any signs of life. There were only cattle and a single farmer cropping in the distance.

Noor finished surveying the empty home and sat in a fit of relief that no one was around. The village did not seem that far and was much larger in the daylight. Noor had only been to that side of the river once in her life. Bourbhan was a settlement, famous for its produce market and beautifully articulated and centered mosque. It's silver dome brought color to the brown buildings, assimilated homes and dirt streets. Gardens surrounded the mosque, and provided an oasis to the city that melded with the deserted farmlands.

Their journey, which had already cost them two days, seemed to be much longer and at the moment a bit odd. Noor could sense no danger and felt that the short walk to Bhourban was to be the easiest part of her journey. Still she knew that anything she took for granted would cost her Mohammed. She went back down to the cellar and retrieved the brown sack. Mohammed was near the mud tossing stones and dried clay. She was about to call upon him, but she heard something she had not heard in quite some time. Laughter. With each stone that bounced into the mud, another grin and another giggle. Noor fizzled at her attempts to gather Mohammed. She watched with each casting motion and each ear-to-ear smile, as Mohammed seemed calm. For the first time in a long time he looked carefree, and his demeanor began to rub off on Noor. But before she got too carried away she knew the only way for him to survive and laugh again, was to make their way across the river and into the silver domed sanctuary.

She reached down for the sack and held it in her hands, the tighter she squeezed the longer she would wait. The more she wanted to call out to Mohammed the more she resisted. It was a cruel gesture to deceive herself of the harmonious possibilities that no longer existed. She stood and waltzed toward Mohammed, and waited until he noticed that she was right behind him. He slowly turned back, looked at the sack, dropped the rock and looked up at his mother.

"We are not so far away anymore." She delicately remarked as she opened the sack.

"Will God forgive me?"

Noor appeared as an effigy, she did not move, and could not comprehend what Mohammed was asking.

"Forgive you for what?" she rhetorically replied.

"Striking down Ehsan. Making him bleed."

"You were protecting your father, you were doing what anyone would do. God forgives those whom act upon good intentions."

Mohammed paused and tried to fathom his mother's words. He wanted to believe, but it was hard knowing that comfort was not being uttered from his fathers mouth. "Will he forgive me for making Abu stay away from us?"

Noor struggled to find the words to comfort Mohammed. "God…God will forgive you."

"Abu will not." He stopped throwing rocks.

Up until that moment Noor had always taken her responsibilities for granted. She was just a child when she gave birth to Mohammed, and already he was growing up quicker than she could imagine. She had known her son to be quiet and smart, but his intuition caught her by surprise. She was upset that she was not with her husband, but did not think to make Mohammed an outlet.

"Do you remember the story of the prophet Ibrahim and his son Ismael? Ibrahim was asked by God to sacrifice Ismael. Ibrahim did not question what he had to do. Instead he took Ismael up atop the hillside and placed him on the stone and was about to kill him, but God switched Ismael with a goat. You did what you had to do. You saw that your father was being attacked and you rushed to help him. You didn't think of Ehsan, or Abdullah, you thought about the one you love and you helped him, you understood that he needed help…Without a doubt in your mind you helped him." She grabbed Mohammed by the shoulders and made him look into her eyes. "You rescued him. I should have done that…but you did. Just as with Ibrahim, God has a plan for us."

"Did he mean for me to turn Abu away?"

"I don't know jaan…I don't know."

Noor felt disturbed. She knew she had raised this child and that he belonged to her, yet there was something about this questioning that separated them. Something that Mohammed kept hidden from her. He was growing into a man before her eyes, a man with little need of a mother. She could speak no words of encouragement, and no words of resolve; she was just a mother and a troubled child. The duties of an Indian mother had fallen from grace, this was a man's territory, one that she had not come to terms with. She felt like she was Mohammed's child in an unfamiliar place.

" I wish Abu were here, he would know what to do."

She put her hands on Mohammed and guided him into the sack. She threw it upon the other side of her shoulder, the side without a fresh cut.

"I can't say."

5

Abass had been gone for quite some time now. Mohammed was already tired, but he made an exception to meet with this stranger and he was not going to tarnish that agreement. Abass entered the room a few minutes later with his pant legs rolled up. They were a little wet.

"I apologize Mohammed, I missed Isha prayer and had to go make it up before I forgot."

"No need my friend. God comes before all else." Mohammed realized that he was late for prayer as well. "Where did you go to pray? I must tend to mine as well." Abass instructed the directions to Mohammed and told him there was a place for absolution as well.

"You did not drink your tea?"

Mohammed smiled and shook his head. "I was waiting for you, but please drink."

"I cannot, I will wait for you. Actually I will send for some new tea while you are gone."

"I will be back shortly."

Mohammed followed Abass' directions down the opposite corridor. His footsteps echoed in the marble hallway. The eerie sound dissipated as he reached the end of the hall and into the absolution room. He was greeted with six white marble seats, nestled under six matching faucets. The room was in the shape of a crescent and two drainage holes at the ends of the room gathered the used water. He entered the room, took off his shoes, socks, loosened his tie and shirt at the wrist and neck, lastly taking off his coat jacket. He crouched down and sat upon the cold hard marble and rolled up the cuffs on his pant legs. The water was cool and felt refreshing upon his hands, then face and arms and finally his feet. The water trickled to the end of the rooms and splashed upon the small marble tiles separating the drainage area from the seats. He walked back to the door and took a towel from the cabinet; he dried himself and leaned against the wall. "Nothing is as clean as a sinner seeking peace."

After gathering his clothing he headed to the prayer room, which was attached to the hotel. "Ironic" he thought to himself, these days mosques were pushed far and away from most anything current. It was actually an inspiring change to Mohammed. He could see that many influences do not reach as far as he thought.

The green carpets within the mosque were slightly separated by the white lines drawn to separate rows of worshippers. Large frames of the words "Allah" and "Islam" and "Peace" were placed above the windows that looked out upon the city. A glass dome in the center was tinted and gave a clear unbiased view of the sky, but more importantly the moon. The light that it cast down seemed like the best place for Mohammed to pray. As he lined up and pronounced the call to prayer, two men entered the mosque and made their way to the Qurans stacked on shelves in the corner. The interruption was abrupt but not major enough to deter Mohammed from continuing.

Prayer itself was not something that seemed to waste Mohammed's time. Rather it gave Mohammed time to slow down and recount his blessings. He knew that it was a time to remember Allah, but he would often stray in his thoughts. He would see his four daughters growing up and getting married. He would look at his son's face and see how much he reminded him of his father. His wife Sophia was the apple of his eye and jewel in his thoughts; she did not ever stray from his mind for more than an hour. He would look upon all the things he did in his life- his childhood, his education in America, his marriage to his younger cousin and their lives beyond his. He prayed to keep his sanity and indulge in his own life. It was selfish. It was wonderful.

Isha prayer usually took him a few minutes, within this time he remembered not to stray for too long. His guest was waiting and he didn't want to stay up any longer than he had to. His request to meet with Mohammed was still a mystery. He made no indication and gave no hint as a possible outline to what he had to discuss. Mohammed hoped that it would not take that long and that it was not a sales pitch for some new land. He missed his family and wanted to hear the comforting voices in Karachi. He had to get to a phone, and call his family. They were asleep, but they were anxious to know where Mohammed had been. One sound of the phone and they knew that it was Mohammed; they would all get up and run to speak to him.

Once he had finished, the men in the corner of the room's conversation began to appeal to him. All he had heard was bits and pieces of the conversation, enough to know that it was about Jihad. He did not want to interrupt the men but he was interested. They flipped through pages and quoted God's word to each other.

"It is not a fight, nor a war." One of the men commented.

"Jihad is protecting yourself and your family from injustice?" The other replied.

It was an unusual conversation to have in the middle of the night. Judging by the clothing and appearance of the two he had deciphered that they were hotel employees.

Mohammed thought to himself: " both of these men are wrong. Jihad is a struggle, any struggle." He told himself. He had many himself. He wanted to approach the men but he did not, instead he greeted them from afar. "As Salaamu Alaikum."

"Walaikum A Salaam." They both replied in unison.

Mohammed got up from his prayer and headed back to the dining hall where his guest was waiting. He did not notice both of the men stare at him on his way out of the mosque.

"Jihad." One of them commented.

The other man just looked upon Mohammed as he exited and looked back at the other and nodded.

Mohammed had made his way out to the hallway that led him to the mosque, he was consumed by the thought of being home, seeing his wife, and conversing with his children. He didn't notice the two gentlemen in the mosque were following behind him. When he went to turn around they were still talking to each other as they exited into an adjacent hall that led out to the entry gate to the hotel.

The men removed keys from their pocket and lined themselves up against two similar silver sedans sitting in the parking lot. They both surveyed the area and got into their cars and made for the exit of the hotel. As one car turned out onto the empty street the other turned the car into the gate and blocked both the entry and the exit. The other car turned and came back toward the hotel. It paused for a moment several feet away from the entry gate, it sat idling as if it were ready to engage. Revving its engine it finally kicked into drive and headed for the other car sitting parallel within the entry gate.

The driver looked at the car blistering its way toward him it drew near quicker and quicker. He did not remove himself instead he sat nervously as he checked his rear view mirror. "Jihad…Indeed." He closed his eyes and gripped hard onto the steering wheel.

6

India 1937

The smell of naan roamed throughout the bazaar streets of Bhourban. The silver dome in the midst of the city was blinding travelers with its spherical reflection. It was just past midday as all the stores had reopened after Zohur prayer. The liveliness of the area awakened again as business went about as usual. Families wandered the street looking for the next bargain, whether it is within a store or by a poor child's hand. The streets interchanged between cement and dirt. The gutter was being cleaned by the untouchables while the higher caste walked above them.

It was familiar to Noor, but she had never been this exposed to the poorer cities. This was in fact Mohammed's first time being around such a different cast of community (although his view was obstructed from within the hemp sack). They were in no hurry to stop and examine the surrounding atmosphere, for they had to make it to the mosque before they could truly calm. They were a few blocks from the crown jewel of a desolate town. It towered among the blocks of homes and drew in vendors of all sorts. Noor and Mohammed made their way to the cement gated entrance. There were hijras that stood outside and begged for money. Other children and women beggars and food vendors flanked them. It seemed that there were more people outside the mosque than were inside. Noor waited outside in hope that she might catch a glimpse of her husband. She looked upon each man's face that passed her by. None held familiar and none held friendly. They waited and waited. Without a sense of time and or placement they blended within the crowd of beggars. Noor did not dare go inside the mosque for fear of retribution and fear of someone recognizing her.

As noon turned to night the street turned from clean to a trash oasis. Blowing debris littered upon the street and gave more work for the exhausted untouchables. There was a whisper spread amongst the town. Nothing was clear but the system of caste was evident. Noor sat outside the mosque and did not notice the pile of refuge that stacked in front of her. She had set herself down upon a curb and rested herself as well as her bag. She was anxious. She was hurt. Now was the time for her to go in search of her love. Noor circled the mosque compound twice looking within the men's section, the shoe section, and the absolution section. She even recruited the help of children passing by to confirm the appearance of her husband. It was to no avail. She had to wait longer for the promises of reunification. She went back to the curb and sat amongst her new peers. Noor was empty. She felt nothing. Sights and sounds would pass through her. She didn't even notice children poking at the sack that contained Mohammed.

"Separation Coming? Two for one!" A child was roaming around selling knick-knacks, souvenirs, and newspapers. His loud alerts seemed to be the only thing that caught any sign of life from Noor. The way Noor looked toward the boy caught his attention as well. He snickered to himself and made his way directly toward her from across the street. He held up flickering lights, spinning tops and a stack of newspaper. He arrived at Noors curb and examined her from burqa to bruised foot.

"Yes ma'am may I interest you in any of these."

Noor looked upon the boy and saw a future Mohammed, she tried to contain her emotions and commented to the boy: "No need."

"Now I know that there is something that might interest you. A bell, a whistle, anything."

"Nothing."

The newspaper within his hand had an odd effect upon Noor. She saw something that she had to investigate. The boy looked at her and noticed she was staring at the newspaper in his hands. Again he sized her up from head to toe. He looked at her ripped burqa, hemp sack, dirty sandals and brown outlined hem. "Oh, you wouldn't be interested in that, you have to be able to read."

"Let me see the newspaper you have."

"Okay, okay that's fifty rupees."

"Fifty rupees! I'll give you 25 and not a cent more."

"Ma'am please, I live on the street and leave nothing for myself except the love of God. Would you be the one to take the food from my mouth? Forty rupees."

"You snide little rascal! You will get nothing more than thirty rupees. Especially for those lies! I see you wearing nice new shoes and the necklace around your neck. You would believe that I wouldn't know about you and the family you have and the home you live in. I should whip the color out of you!"

"…Here take it. Thirty rupees." He handed the newspaper to Noor after snatching the money from out of her hands.

"For another 10 rupees I can read it for you."

Noor raised the backside of her left hand and brought it to the right side of her head as she threatened to slap the boy. He quickly became a memory. She watched as he dispersed into the crowd then turned her attention to the paper.

The words jumped off the paper.

"LAND SPLIT PROPOSED."

She felt the color dissipate from her hands. Her trembling presence remained unnoticed by Mohammed. Life seemed to pass within Noor as an empty shell that washed upon a vast sea. She knew were she had been but was lost upon where to go. Even though Mohammed was with her she was alone. She lied on the ground and stared up at the dome atop the mosque.

Mohammed could see his mother's stature fade like the light. He thought maybe she had seen Ali but he did not recognize her. But he looked at the yellowish news report that flattened against the road. He didn't know what to make of it instead he began jostling in the sack and tried to poke a hole to get a better look. A little rip provided him with his peephole to gather his mother's frustration. He looked in her hands and read the same words. The same effect did not cross Mohammed. It wasn't grief or anger or even sadness. It was something else something he had not felt in quite some time; something that his parents did not feel for the time that Ravinder and Ehsan were alive. He was compelled to jump free from the sack and embrace his mother and comfort her. He tried to open the top and get out, but was promptly denied freedom from his mother tying the knot atop even tighter. She looked toward the sack and shook her head.

"It's still not safe. I will let you out when we find a hidden place."

Mohammed thought her words would encourage her to find a place for him to get up and out. She did not make an effort, she didn't move from her spot at all. Noor just waited and waited for time to ease the shock. Her son became distant. She, however, was still caught within. Hours seemed liked days and the night welcomed a light mist. It roamed the street and entered uninvited into the homes on the ground level. Noor and Mohammed were still amidst the curb waiting for some miracle. As loud as the morn had been it brought no solace of silence with the night. Time evaporated after the final call to prayer sung. Bazaars closed but mouths kept open. Noor had no choice but to take Mohammed into the mosque and find some peace and maybe some ease.

The first step into the mosque was partitioned for men and women. Noor noticed men walking and talking and even sleeping in the confines of the prayer area. She went in search of the women's locale and even more insistent, a corner. A dark one. One to lie out Mohammed and her and wait until the morning rang that brought her a new light and new hope. She walked until she found a secluded area where the shoes were taken off for prayer. The empty pews of shoe racks nestled together to bring a forest of large wooden rectangles. The corner that Noor picked was far from anyone. The closest person was a woman that was reading the Quran and praying without distraction in the illuminated women's prayer section.

Noor nestled the hemp sack against an opaque wall. She opened the top of the sack and tapped the top of Mohammed's head. She didn't realize that she exposed Mohammed to darkness from darkness. He was stretching and making his way around his mother's vicinity when he stopped and tried to analyze his new abode. He saw the light shine down on the only woman sitting and praying. He turned his attention to his mother and saw the sorrow in her eyes. He knew that they were to meet with his father and that they were to make their way to Karachi from that point. He was still nowhere to be found and there was no future meeting planned with him. His silence was ascribed toward his mother; it was the only thing that could comfort her. Without word he backed away further into the dark corner and laid awake staring into the abysmal ceiling; welcoming the morn. They both did not speak and stayed awake hoping for a promising future.

"Allahuakbar Allahuakbar!" The force of voice used in the call to prayer bellowed throughout the mosque and into the ears of Noor and Mohammed. Their hidden abode had opened to public traffic quickly. They had gotten no rest and were determined to use the day to their ideas of hope. Mohammed saw the women enter the shoe area. He looked to his mother and immediately made for the flattened sack. Before he was able to enter Noor grabbed hold of his arm and shook her head. It was strange to Mohammed. He had gotten used to closed confines of the sack but wanted to walk the streets with his mother.

"I won't make you go back in the sack. God will protect us as long as we are in the mosque. God will protect us." Noor's voice had a hint of optimism disguised by distress. "I want you to go to the men's area for prayer. Look for you're after prayer, but do not leave the mosque after prayer. We will meet back here at the entrance."

Noor's strategy was strange to Mohammed. However she knew that she had to do anything to instill courage within him to continue.

The mosque was one of the largest buildings Mohammed had ever seen. He didn't know why his mother trusted him walking amongst strangers; he just knew that he couldn't leave her without faith or trust. His first duty was to act upon the Morning Prayer. The mosque revealed itself to him. It spaced itself with the chorus of men and women segregating to make prayer. Candles and generators throughout the fanned prayer halls cast false lighting. Mohammed followed other men through arched hallways cast with white alabaster. The prayer hall itself was enormous- far bigger than the woman's section. It stretched farther than necessary for the amount of people gathered for this prayer. A system of ropes and pulleys provided an air flow scheme with fans alienated every few feet. Large pillars that seemed to reach to the heavens obstructed any clear view of the women's area.

Mohammed noticed men shuffling in and out of two neighboring doors on the other side of the prayer hall. He followed their footsteps to discover the absolution room where he cleaned himself for prayer. Back in the prayer room he made his way to the front of the mosque where rows of men had lined up for duty and forgiveness. Mohammed was in the second line of men directly behind the Imam. Everyone was sitting while the Imam gave a sermon and blessing before he began the prayer.

"God has laid a foundation for men to follow. We are the providers for our women and children. We are strong and must set an example for them. Praying five times a day with sunnah is a must. If we do not instill these values within our families and our communities Shaythan will snatch our lives from us."

The lines behind Mohammed began to fill with men just now making their way to the floor. Still it was no amount to fill the colossal space opened by the mosque.

"Allah is our savior there is only one God and Mohammed is his Messenger. We must remember that when we were first set to pray the number of times set was far greater than five. Mohammed visited God to seek the future of the Muslim's and the manner of remembrance it started with one hundred prayers a day and than was eventually lowered to five. It could have been lowered even more but Mohammed feared that if it were than prayer would be forgotten all together. That is why we must make the most of these prayers. It is a duty and a gift that we fulfill the requirements laid forth by Allah."

The Imam looked about and saw that he was not reaching his audience. They were tired and they were anxious to get on with their day. He rolled his eyes and commenced with a blessing as he cupped both hands and brought them together. With every blessing that was uttered from his mouth a chorus of deep voices followed with 'Ameen.' Mohammed blanked out each blessing he remained silent until he realized that these blessing were catered for him.

"God grant us peace!"

"…Ameen." Mohammed whispered

"God grant us patience!"

"Ameen." Mohammed's voice was not nearly as loud as the other men's.

"God forgive our transgressions!"

"Ameen." Mohammed's voice began to pick up and match the chorus.

"God forgive our misdeeds!"

"Ameen!" He was on the verge of screaming it from his lungs.

"May God forgive us from our sins we have cast upon others!"

Mohammed was silent. He didn't respond that time and didn't until the blessing was finished. The chorus continued on without Mohammed until the Imam decided it was time to commence with Fajr. He signaled to the men to stand up and align themselves to begin prayer. Mohammed stayed sitting and silent. The man next to Mohammed had to pat Mohammed on the shoulder to get him to stand and ready for prayer. Mohammed stood while the call to prayer was sounded again to get the stragglers and the lazy to arrive and join prayer.

It was one of the longer prayers that Mohammed had ever done. He was focused on the idea of finding his father and cheering up his mother. He did not focus as intently as usual and as preached. When the prayer was over each man turned his head to the right and then left shoulder to end their prayer. The man next to Mohammed extended his hand and shook it then got up and left.

The Imam turned back toward the mass and fiddled with his rosary. It looked like he was personally examining each member to see the pureness of his heart and intentions. With each new stare he mumbled something to himself. Mohammed couldn't tell if it was a prayer or the sign of someone who had lost touch with himself. He looked angry and distraught, not a good sign for a believer to witness among a religion that means 'peace.' He continued to scrutinize every man in the line as they would get up off the floor and make for the shoe section and eventually the exit. Mohammed wanted very much to leave before the Imam would look at him. Mohammed checked the hall to see that the numbers were dwindling and now was the time to make for his mother. As the Imam looked in Mohammed's direction Mohammed immediately got up and walked with two other men to the shoe section. He did not know for sure but it seemed that he was being followed. Mohammed was sure he was the last out to the shoe section but he knew he heard footsteps behinds him. He didn't want to give his mother away so he faked making his way to the exit. He grabbed someone else's shoes and walked to the exit. His mothers words did not seem to stop him, he had to distract this follower before his mother was found.

The sun had just peaked the horizon and was blinding the streets with the fog. It was a ghostly scene outside the mosque. The fog that had crept up at night had engulfed the light as bright clouds blocked clear views. Mohammed quickly put on the stolen shoes and walked to the gate and the street. The wooden floors turned marble echoed the footsteps behind him. They were getting louder and they were getting quicker. Mohammed's walk turned into jog he was making his way to the maze of a bazaar. It was big and it was confusing; easy to get lost in; easy to be lost. Stores were just now opening as shop owners were converting their beds into front desks. Mohammed was now running he could sense that no matter how far he ran the footsteps would follow. At the end of the bazaar and back near the mosque was a corner that Mohammed had spotted on his way into the maze. He immediately ran as fast as he could and hid in the corner. The footsteps ceased after just a few seconds. He peered back through the corridor down the bazaar. It was full of families cleaning the outside of their respective stores and stalls. No one seemed to be in pursuit; it was strictly business. Before Mohammed was in the clear a shadowy figure appeared and grabbed hold of him.

"Mohammed!" The familiar voice cried. "Mohammed, my Mohammed!" The voice was not harsh. Instead it was inviting. His face appeared as the sun was still making its climb into the sky.

"Abu!? Abu! Where have you been?"

Ali got down on his knees and held Mohammed close. He did not speak while checking to make sure that Mohammed had not been harmed.

"Where is your mother? Why are you not hidden?"

Mohammed seized hold of his father. Ali picked him up and looked into his eyes. Mohammed then signaled toward the mosque. Ali wasted no time heading in the pointed direction. He held Mohammed with a tight grasp all the way. He wanted to stop and talk to him but that was a matter for the whole family. They got to the mosque and Mohammed was set to the ground but still held by his hand. As they both straightened themselves they noticed that they were being watched.

Noor was standing a few meters away from the two she did not run as she imagined. She was not even relieved. The headlines on the newspaper kept pounding their words into her thoughts.

"Noor, come."

She did not budge. Ali had no choice but to take hold of her arm and pick up Mohammed. She tried fighting loose but was denied by the fierce grasp Ali had placed. After continually trying to free herself she began to tire. She looked at the people they passed looking at them and see her struggling. None took exception and stepped in to help. She looked down and let Ali guide her. Mohammed in the meanwhile was more concerned with being with his father. He did not remove his sight from him; his relief came from his comfort. Mohammed took both of them into the bazaar toward a small hostel hidden within. A small room in the back had already held most of Ali's traveling materials. He set Mohammed down on the small bed on the floor and pushed Noor in the corner near the non-partitioned bathroom. Ali slammed the door shut and locked it.

Ali pulled a chair from out of an open and broken closet. He sat down and sighed, then looked up at Noor and Mohammed. He was nervous, too nervous. He was granted no comfort by Noor and didn't want any from Mohammed. The tension between the three soon choked the lifeless room. Ali took Mohammed by the hand and escorted him into a connected room. "Stay here." He shut and locked the door and left Mohammed to himself.

"Wait." Mohammed muffled through the door.

Back on the other side Ali was still holding the doorknob. His forehead was pressed against the door, and his body was flimsy. Noor had to see what he was concealing. It would've been right to hide it from her but she had to know in order to forgive Ali. He felt in his coat pocket, the long sliver piece still with him and the consequences it held. He pulled it out and held it in his hands, and then he took off the cap. The ink was leaking. Ali checked his pocket again and breathed a sigh of relief; the ink had bled onto his jacket and for the most part avoided a more valuable asset. He took out the paper and handed it to Noor. "Read it." Noor took the paper and unfolded it, her eyes grazed the words and she looked back at Ali.

Mohammed could only make out muffled words and a few yells, but nothing that he could determine himself. He could make out his father's voice, but could barely hear his mother's words. The only words he could clearly make out was 'Abdullah.' It was just noise after a while, one that became a lullaby for Mohammed. He fought his way to sleep as the noise died down about an hour later. Mohammed didn't notice as he was falling asleep, he couldn't hold a thought for longer than his eyes remained open. Suddenly the sound of the door unlocking raised his senses again. He got up and ran to the door and pushed it open. He found his father and mother sitting within each other's embrace at the end of the bed. His mother did not look depressed but there was no hint of joy. His father just nodded and presented Mohammed with the same face that had annoyingly become accustomed. The dust in the room outlined the light pillars shining through a tattered window cover. Mohammed felt he had to speak or at least ask what they talked about, but he knew his distance, and he knew his place.

They were a family again, for the most part.

7

December 18, 1973

Mohammed always got a second wind from prayer. This night was strange as it held no purpose but only a promise. Abass was the most familiar face that Mohammed had around him. He was on his way back from making prayer and was no longer tired. Instead he was adamant about receiving his guest's attention and request. He had made this hotel a home to welcome an odd and edgy guest. This was one of his last days in Islamabad and he didn't want to leave unheard. He paused at the bottom of a staircase and examined the beautiful sweep it created. He marveled at the way it disappeared from afar and came into view once you looked for it. It was pure black and intersected at the top of a white platform several feet above.

Mohammed once planned something as beautiful as this for a library in Karachi. It took him weeks to develop and months to plan. He spent time and money away from his family and his newborn and only son. He remembered the day his idea was abruptly overruled and thrown out. A new mall was to be resurrected across the street from another one. No one wanted education these days, it was all commercial. Corporations held more sway over communities then self ideals and prosperity. It still brought him shame, to say that his country would rather hold a shopping bag in their hands than a degree.

"Mohammed it is hard to pry you away from anything structural." Abass snuck his way beside Mohammed.

"Not hard just…well I guess hard would be the right word." Mohammed checked his watch and saw that he was gone for more than thirty minutes. "Excuse my absence."

"I will do no such thing. God comes before all else."

They walked back toward the dining hall.

"You seem to be more comfortable now. Such a profound effect prayer has on us."

"Indeed."

"So Abass. Tell me what was it that you wanted to present to me?"

"Well…Sahib."

His stature and presentational manner gave away the fact that he was practicing this for a long time.

"I am not from a well off family such as yours. I do not hold a high education such as you. The town I come from is poor and is in dire need of your potential. "

"You are not from Islamabad?"

"A small town outside Peshawar sir."

"That is a long way from here."

"It is indeed a long walk."

•

Mohammed hated to admit it but he loved to accompany anyone that sought knowledge. Somehow he knew that Abass knew this.

Abass continued with his speech. "My family and neighbors do not have access to anything of educational value. I am afraid that the next generation will follow in my footsteps and take a low paying job to survive. Children will be torn from literacy and turned to cheap shop keepers and beggars. If there was a school and even a library that would turn our fortunes."

"Why me Abass? There are so many people in Islamabad that would help you find your way and build with your community."

"Not true Sahib. Everyone that we have contacted was not interested in such a low paying long-timing project."

"Well if it is a school that should take no time at all."

"That is not what we were told."

"Wait, wait, wait. Peshawar? There are schools there already and I know there is a library."

"Umm…yes…well you see sir there is more to education to the common land owner. It is a commodity for the rich and those with money. Nothing is free. We must pay for our children to attend, not to mention the extra taxes placed upon us for their schools. The prices are outrageous for a shop owner or farmer that can make no savings."

The two entered the dining hall and sat at the desk. The tea was gone but the cups and side dishes were bunched empty next to each other. They sat down in their chairs and signaled to the host outlining the kitchen.

Mohammed had been dealing with enough businessmen and authorities to know that this meeting was more than just a proposal. The hidden agenda had not yet become apparent but Mohammed was still going to try.

"What exactly are you proposing to me Abass?"

"To open a public school and conjoined library headed by you in agreement with us."

"Public?" The idea tugged at Mohammed's heart. "Most schools in that area are private?"

"Almost all. We have to invest our children in our work to scarcely break even."

"Let me ask you something Abass? If I were to help plan and build this school and library, how would that change the fact that you and your peers need money?"

"Many of us have thought about that. We would sacrifice our standard of living to increase our childrens."

Mohammed was in the presence of someone of his father's nature. "That is admirable Abass." He sighed and thought about the past. "If you will allow me to speak plainly then…I once had this same opportunity to build a school on the outskirts of Karachi. The families spoke in the same manner and the children were as promising as any I had ever seen before."

"Then surely you will help."

Mohammed continued. "I built this school and the promise arose and the children and families were happy. Do you know what happened next Abass? The school became a shelter and was split into different homes. It was eventually and collectively scrapped for building materials and raw land. The children went back to work a few years later and the parents went to someone else and asked the very same deed. Do you know what I am asking Abass? I would gladly do this, but there has to be more than just a promise, there has to be a united belief and understanding. An educating institution is the best gift that any parent could wish for their child. I would have never thought to write up a legal agreement if it weren't for that instance but if I were to do this that is my accord."

"An agreement Sahib?"

"Yes. That I will provide the teachers, I will provide the books, materials, play area, and syllabus. You and your peers however will continue to provide the children. If that accord is broken or remotely digressed then I will have your taxes increased."

"Sahib?"

"I take education very seriously. That is one of the main purposes for our innocence in childhood; it is for us to learn. Unfortunately for you and I, our education now comes from our mistakes and I do not make the same mistakes twice."

"I will present this idea to the community."

"Make sure you do, I will give you everything you need to get in contact with me if my end of the bargain is met."

"Yes. Sahib."

The rushed agreements and responses did not make a believer out of Mohammed. As he looked at Abass, the nervousness that had subsided earlier seemed to return.

"Tell me something Abass. You do not strike me as someone that comes from the North."

"Oh Sahib." Abass' laugh did not convince Mohammed. "I often hear that when I am in Islamabad."

He dithered then persisted. "…I come from a family that was originally from Lahore."

There was something suspicious about his quality to Mohammed. "Oh. Lahore! I am from Lahore." He lied. "Where in Lahore."

"Oh indeed. Um… well it is on the north side next to Bhamma."

"So you are from Bhamma?"

"Yes."

"Where in Bhamma?"

"Oh…It's been a long time. But near… Service Road."

"Well Service Road is a very long road, you will have to be more specific."

"Right near Service and Bhamma Road."

"Indeed." Mohammed's questions were amusing to him, but it seemed that his badgering demoralized Abass.

The host reemerged from the twin dining doors leading into the kitchen. The teapot in his hands was covered by a bamboo mat and balanced by his bare hand. He arrived at the table and poured the steaming tea into their cups. The host nodded to Mohammed and then looked Abass in the eyes and nodded. Mohammed went for the sugar and cream.

"How do you take yours Abass?"

"One sugar Sahib."

Mohammed obliged Abass then treated himself. As he stirred he crossed his legs and waited for Abass to break the silence. It was Mohammed's unusual and effective way to incur a hidden response. Abass' intuition was no match for Mohammed's tactic. They both sat in a stalemate stirring and staring waiting for the other to break first. Abass waited but Mohammed's quickly raised eyebrows and smirk did not help his cause.

"This tea is very good." Abass remarked.

"Indeed. The stories are true."

Mohammed looked at his watch again. There was no need to continue this cat and mouse game. He didn't want to admit it, but he wanted Abass to be demoralized by his questioning and the agreement of the school. It didn't have the intended effect but it did deter Abass from continuing.

The tea was coming to the black grain that separated from bags used to brew. Abass was waiting for Mohammed to finish drinking before he sipped at his tea.

Mohammed had not noticed that Abass didn't even take a taste of his tea. He was trying to end this meeting so that he could make the call to his family. Abass was not what he had sized him up to be. He was not impressed by his sudden agreement and immediate withdrawal. He finished his tea and sighed, he wished there was more for at least the tea would provide him with humbleness.

"Now was there anything else Abass?"

"…No…Sahib."

"If you would allow me to take my leave. It is getting late and I do have an early start tomorrow."

Abass was still shocked at the sudden turn of events. "Absolutely."

"Please leave your information at the front desk if you still wish to get in contact in the future."

The host came out of the kitchen and Mohammed signaled to him to bring the check. As was customary between grown Pakistani men Abass quickly interrupted him.

"No please Mohammed, let me."

"My friend there is no need. I will take care of this."

"No! It was my honor to have you as my guest. Please."

Mohammed stood and offered his hand to shake. Abass paused for a second to look at his hands then stood and received him. Mohammed nodded after the handshake and made his way back to the hall and to the stairwell. He looked back and saw Abass sit back down; oddly he did not make for the exit. Instead the host accompanied him. Mohammed watched as the host shook Abass' hand as he turned the corner. He was so anxious to get to his room that he didn't think to turn back and receive the host, whom was so patient with him. He opened the door to the stairwell and looked up. The ten floors he had to climb seemed like the scale of the karakoram mountain range.

8

India, 1942

Karachi was as beautiful as it was abstract as it was busy. There was a swing in the shade that often cast over city by heavy pollution caused by the ship tankers nestled to the south of the city. It was developed as quickly as it was promised, but a promise that was created to quick to be afterthought. Streets had no signs and the only way to get somewhere was if you knew where you were going, or where you had been. It was like Bhourbhan only a thousand times larger and a lot busier. People walked with a purpose and conducted their daily routines just as so. The dusk would bring in the promise of no stars, as the dawn would gather shreds of light to awaken the guttered suburbs.

To Mohammed this city looked as if it were thrown together overnight. It was as if people entered and settled where they pleased. It was good to see that family tied no one or indulged blood rights. He could see this city was ripe for the taking and his mind only grew with his appetite to follow in his father's footsteps. The window where he stood gave Mohammed an eagle's view of the city from the outskirt of the eastern side to the ocean shore that held it prisoner. He always dreamed this would be a view set from his office, not from a hospital bedroom.

His view was shaded. His family had been in Karachi for a few years. Mohammed was ready for college and ready to leave Pakistan, his father however was not fit to leave his deathbed, nor his mother to leave his side. Mohammed was not ready to give his family the news of college acceptance in distant lands. His family was well off enough to live without him, they had always been. His only fear was leaving his mother completely alone. Although it had been quite sometime since they had migrated west, the time he and his mother spent gave him further reason to enter into a higher education. Aside from the usual sonly duties, his interactions with his mother seemed forced by his father. He no longer needed to be comforted or held. His prowess came from the strength he observed in his father. There were never any indications of true love between Noor and Ali other than smiling and holding hands. Part of that limit seemed to rub off on Mohammed toward the main woman in his life. He knew it would be difficult to leave her alone, but the fact was they only lived for each other through Ali.

"Mohammed." His father called. "By the way you look out that window it would seem you are more keen to visit the city, than your dying father."

"Abu, don't say such things. You know you are going to be better, this city needs you after all."

"Ha, this city was never mine for the taking. It is now yours to look over. Come sit here." Ali signaled to the end of the bed. "Tell me of the schools you have applied to."

"Abu I've told you ten times already which schools."

"Yes. Yes you have. Have you told your mother?"

"I don't think that is something she wants to hear."

"It is. It is. I cannot seem to define the rift between you two."

"Rift?" Mohammed questioned.

"Yes. Ever since we left India there was something that happened. Is there anything that you want to tell me?"

"No. Because there is nothing."

"Make sure you are here for your mother. Let her know you will take care of her."

Mohammed stayed silent waiting for his father to change the subject. 'She always needs someone to watch over her?' Mohammed thought to himself. It shamed him to see that weakness evident in his family. "Abu I thought that we were talking about schools?"

"Ah yes. Then perhaps you can indulge me and let me know which ones you want to attend."

His father's tone was joking, but his manner was far more serious. The sore subject of leaving him and his mother alone never really gained any momentum. The fact was Ali was not to last for longer than four days. Mohammed knew it. Noor denied it. Ali embraced it.

"Well there is Osmania University."

"Yes. Yes. My Alma Mater."

"Then there is Cambridge and the University of Pennsylvania as well."

"Fine schools my boy. Fine schools."

"There is however one that I wanted to let you and amma know about."

"Cornell?"

Mohammed was shocked he didn't know his father knew. He should've known though, Ali had not stopped talking about what could have been when he was a prospective college boy. His father denied him the chance to uphold a dream of traveling to America. He felt he would know that this was his one chance.

"Yes Abu. Cornell."

Ali took Mohammed by the hand and sat up in his bed.

"No matter what the choice make sure that it is something that pleases you. I know that you do not want to stay here to go to college. That is the experience of college itself: to know a world outside that of your own. To live by means not provided by your mother or me. That is how we come into adulthood, which is how you will know you are ready to start your own family. Choose a college but let it be a choice you are content with not something that has died by a former dream of mine." He squeezed Mohammed's hand tighter. "Just…just please let me know what you plan to do before I die."

The door to the room was cracked open and suddenly opened. A vast array of family members poured into the room with gifts and flowers. They were all dressed in black. They already assumed the worst. It was that time of the week when relatives would crowd the room and falsely convey rhythms of hope. It was unnatural to Mohammed. His family would gather for cause of death but was separated by the variances in life. He was saddened by the truth, but was grateful his father inspired this conformity. Mohammed stepped away from the bed and made his slow escape to the hall. He managed to step one foot out into the hall before nearly knocking a scurrying woman to the ground.

"Oh. Pardon me. I am sorry."

"Oh. You must be Mohammed."

"I am."

"Salaam, I am your aunt from Goulshan."

Mohammed had only ever met her once and that was the first time they received guests for their arrival to Karachi.

Noor made her way around the corner and she was holding the hand of two small children. She brought them to the door and signaled them to sit outside the room and wait. She turned to Mohammed and gestured to his aunt. "You remember your poupoo jaan right."

"Of course."

"These are her two beautiful girls. Sophia and Rana. Aren't they beautiful Mohammed?"

He was shocked by his mothers mood swing. He suspected it was due to the family surrounding. Nonetheless he looked upon the two girls. Rana was as cute as any child her age should be, bubbly, without a care in the world. He turned his attention to Sophia. She had struck Mohammed. She was young but held a beauty that was far superior to her age. He was stuck staring and deducing each facet of her face. Her long black hair and almond shaped eyes. Her nose was pierced and hands were small but masked by henna. She was quite young but he still couldn't help himself look beyond and see what was to become of her beauty. How could a child this young hold such a presence? He was glad his mother had made the comment of being beautiful because his place was now to observe rather than comment.

"Well Mohammed, aren't they?"

"Yes. Very much so." He looked at his aunt. "They take after their mother."

"That's what your mother said." She said blushing.

Noor crawled back into her shell and presented herself in a different manner as she began to show Mohammed's aunt into the hospital room. Mohammed shook his gaze from Sophia and walked toward the stairwell at the end of the hall. He didn't stop to get approval nor go back into the room to meet with his family. This was a time for grieving only his he and his father were aware of that point. The pretense introduced by his family sickened him, and caused him to relapse into a world outside theirs. He loved his distant family but couldn't bare their presence while his family lay stricken. He made his way to the entrance and waited outside in harmony while the parade of ignorance titled around his father. He needed solace, he was selfish for doing so, but he needed it. He looked across the bustling street and made for the shwarma stand that hid underneath movie advertisements. His intentions did not go unnoticed as his mother followed him.

Noor waited until Mohammed had settled himself across the street then made her way to him. She stood behind him until her presence was noticed.

"Oh amma, why are you not with the others?"

"I am here with you. Isn't that good enough?"

"Of coarse but shouldn't you be with the others and Abu?"

"I should be asking you that same question. What are you doing out here, you know your father needs you right now. I need you right now."

"I just needed some air."

"It has always been that way with us hasn't it? All the answers in life you seek through your father while all the comfort I seek is through him as well."

"We are both very selfish with him."

"I know in my heart that he will pass, just as you and I eventually will. But don't let your emotions shade you from being there for him…and me."

Mohammed was surprised his mother was being so straightforward. It encouraged his thoughts of her growing independence.

"I am here for you amma."

"Are you? I just saw you sulk away from your family."

"I can't be with them right now."

"Why not?"

"I just can't. I can't stand the sight of them right now."

"Why? What have they done? What is the meaning of your anger towards them?"

"They have don—"

"What! Tell me. Did they hurt you did they wrong you in some way."

"No its just that—"

"What is it jaan? Just tell me?"

Mohammed was impressed by his mother's forceful attitude. "Why are they here now? Where were they when we fled Hyderabad? Where were they when we had to stray for our lives? Where were you when—" He caught himself before continuing on. He could see his mother caught that very important word.

"I know it was hard for you to comprehend the idea of being left with your weak mother. Don't make yourself a martyr for our survival. Yes, I didn't know how to help you survive without your father, but we made it. Regardless of how hard it was on us, we made it through that time, and with each other we will make it through this, God willing." She waited a few moments before continuing. "The family that was not there for us then is here for us now. And while we were not there for each other back then we are now." She leant over and kissed Mohammed's forehead. "It is up to you to make the most of it." She walked back to the hospital.

Mohammed waited until darkness cued the streetlights and signaled for his family members leave the hospital, and rush to dinner in their safe, healthy, and comforting homes. Finally the cue came and just like he prophesized his family came strolling out of the hospital. He rushed back across the street and to his father. His mother sat in the corner reading the Quran, rocking back and forth, paused to greet him. His father had a radio nuzzled next to him. It was just background noise while he read the newspaper. Mohammed was discovered as soon as he entered the room.

"Why do you leave whenever they come? I would like you by my side at all times." His father said while stilling eyeing the paper. "They are your family, they are here to give us their prayers."

"Is that what we are calling it now? It's a shame Abu! They only conceive this plan to see you because you are the richest one. They do it to save themselves."

Ali reached lowered his paper and the volume of the radio. "I can understand why you run away when you feel angry. It is admirable you wouldn't want us to see that."

"I wasn't running away. I was jus—"

"Then why are you really angry?"

Mohammed glanced at his mother who was still looking at the Quran but did not her eyes. "How am I supposed to stand here and give thanks for what God has given you. That is why they are here isn't it? To give thanks that you are suffering. To feel better about how they live their lives and how when you are gone they will come to us for land! To witness a man upon his deathbed! Are you dying, are you living? They come and present you life Abu in small children and open smiles. You should be the only one smiling Abu! You can leave this world and embrace God while leaving us to his deceit."

"Mohammed you are beyond your bounds!" Noor interrupted.

Mohammed looked at her then put his head down. He was more in awe of her new ambiance. "Sorry amma. Sorry abu."

Ali looked at Noor and asked her to leave the room. He waited until she closed the door and calmly signaled for Mohammed to continue.

"To look in the face of death and offer it prayer and solace! I am not a pawn Abu! And neither are you or amma." His lashing was brutal, and much to his discourse, overdue.

"We are all pawns my son. Some of us have use to deeds beyond our needs. Perhaps my whole life was meant just for you to understand this very moment. If it is not faith in God you have, then look elsewhere. Faith is not compromised, it is beaten and broken, that is how it will grow in you. I have given you the clues through myself, you have to take those and make them your own. Your anger does not fall upon deaf ears. I know that we don't interact with our family as often as I would like, but that is my doing not theirs or yours."

"Then how am I supposed to feel if it was your failure as a duty?"

"Feel…feel weightless, and let it serve as a reminder of where your anger resides."

"Very well Abu…Cornell."

"Cornell?"

"Yes I have decided."

"I know."

"How?"

"Your face, demeanor. You forget that I am a businessman as well as your father. Also the fact that you kept it from us for so long."

"How long?"

"From the minute it was in your mind as a child. These other places- you didn't want to go there. You wanted us to be led astray, didn't you?"

"No. I-"

"Your mother and I always knew you were smart, from the moment you started to read we could not pry you away from your studies. Not even for the most important occasions… Maybe it's a good thing I'm dying."

"I always did as you taught."

"Don't let your anger deceive you. You did it for yourself. You always had persistence for your own advance and the growth for your indulgences…many see it as selfish and weak." He cleared his throat and spoke. "It is neither."

Ali called back to Noor who was sitting outside of the hospital room; she heard everything but was waiting to be back with her husband. She came back to his side and held his right arm.

Mohammed sat in his mother's chair and looked at his father. The lights of Karachi spread farther than hinted by the day would suggest. Mohammed stayed seated in the chair and picked up his mother's Quran and began to skim through it. Noor stood by Ali's side they remained calm and hushed as they stood looking into each other's eyes, without a word, without a tension. Mohammed spent the next half and hour looking up passages in the Quran he was taught in grade school. He didn't notice his father and mother's unmoving devotion. The words in the Quran rocked him slowly to sleep away from his anger, his mother, and at last his father for the last time.

9

"Ladies and Gentlemen." The voice on the speakers was echoing throughout the quad. "Please join me in accepting…" The day was cloudy yet comfortable. It was much colder than was accustomed to Mohammed in Karachi. "The Cornell graduating class of…" Mohammed was alone and in a foreign country on the greatest day thus far of his short life. His emotions were a hodgepodge of happiness and relief mixed with pain and anxiety. He was in the midst of balancing offers from American and British companies mixed with the (in comparison) humble offer from the State of Pakistan.

"Mohammed. Mohammed. Stand up." A tugging at his arm pulled him back to reality.

"What is it?"

"We all have to stand and accept our degrees."

New York was in the midst of its most beautiful spring bloom. It was fitting that the hard work for years was being handed out on a day like this.

Mohammed rose to his feet and copied his peers as he shuffled in succinct motion toward the right.

"By the way did you review the offer from my father's company?"

Mohammed laughed as he was just weighing the options in his head.

"Your father would seem to have more use with you than myself."

"I told you, why don't you let me take that offer in Pakistan, you can live here and work with my father's company. It works out for everyone."

"Do I detect a hint of concern?"

"You know my father. He is in love with you. He would step over his own son just to have you part of his firm. If he weren't married I would think he was in love with you the way he always mentions your name during breakfast, lunch, and dinner."

"I know I thought about it for hours every night, his offer is intriguing and New York is unlike any place in the world."

"Then stay. Think of the times you and I will have. It will be just like these days all over again!"

"Marcus, its not that I wouldn't want to work for him its just I want to get as far away from you as possible."

They both laughed as the voice began to announce names. Since it was the Graduate Class that was being called they were to take the most time and prestige calling out achievements along with the names. The line was approaching the stage and the students were again shifted back into single lines. Mohammed noticed the applause awarded each person during his or her moment of fame. This class was small not many people had gone into or made it through the Masters Program for Architecture at Cornell. They were the few and the bold, they were survivors being handed their meal ticket.

"Michael Abber." The voice pronounced alound.

Mohammed had waited six years for this moment, the moment where he could declare his triumph in a foreign country and return as a hero to his country. He was the first Pakistani man to graduate with a degree in architecture at Cornell. His father's words still held true with him.

"Terrence Addison."

His time was drawing nearer and it his fifteen minutes were ready to be uncovered. The line moved in front of him.

"Get ready my friend." Marcus coached from behind him.

"Mohammed Ahmed." He was more surprised that his name was properly pronounced. Then it kicked in; he walked to the center of the stage in the Arts Quad and was warmly greeted by applause and faculty. He walked directly to the announcer and detoured to the table with his Professor. He reached his hand and trembled as he squeezed the degree with his mind. His professor quickly withdrew it for he had a few words before Mohammed's future was handed over to him.

"Well Mohammed here we are. Do you remember the first thing I said to you when I met your class?"

It was his final, final exam.

"Indeed. The world is structurally unsound."

"Very good." He grinned and handed him his hard work. "Best of luck in the future."

He walked to the side and into a dark corner created by the makeshift stage set in the autumn background. He opened it, the gold from within was like a treasure being uncovered. The words jumped from within and into his mind.

He couldn't help but remember his father and the day he was buried. He spoke through the grave and to his father's spirit. He watched as his body was lowered into the sacred and ancient ground. The conversation he held with him outlined his return when his education was completed. The most important promise he made to his father was fulfilled. He was ready to make his life his own.

Marcus surprised him and jumped onto his back. The force nearly jostled his degree to the ground. "It's official! We did it."

"Now it's time for you to go meet your parents."

"No. No. It is time for us to meet my parents."

"I can't. I have to go call my mother first."

"That can wait, I promised my father and mother that I would bring you to them."

Mohammed was flattered, but he often felt that their obsession with him was that of a zookeeper to an animal. He was exotic and a childlike fascination. Although they were very kind, he was not a fool. He could see past their ploy. He was often invited as the only foreigner to their extravagant parties and dinner receptions. It was partly the reason why he did not want to stay and work for his father. He was a topic of discussion and amusement for lifeless and bored. He would however pamper Marcus for he had been a true friend. They came out of the quad and out toward a pale Rolls Royce. The driver emerged from the car and opened the passenger door. Out stepped a painfully mature woman drenched in fur and a pearl outlined hat. Followed by a well-groomed and dressed debonair man in a tuxedo holding a cigar about to be lit. It was always an odd match to Mohammed, for Marcus' father seemed much younger than his mother was. Marcus approached his mother and father and hesitated for an embrace.

"Excellent work boy." His father unenthusiastically commented.

"Yes Marcus you have done quite adequately." His mother was a little more convincing.

They both looked past Marcus and to Mohammed who was standing a little farther behind.

"There he is, what a fine job you have done, Mohammed. You didn't tell me of all your academic achievements. Where did you get the time after working on such an impressive portfolio?" Marcus' father walked up to him and heftly shook his hand.

"Thank you Mr. Beacon. I have you and Mrs. Beacon to thank for you hospitality."

"Think nothing of it. In fact…" He gathered closer to Mohammed and led him on a short walk. "Did you have time to look into my offer?"

"I did."

"And?"

"You are very generous Mr. Beacon. However…" Mohammed paused and was copied by Mr. Beacon. "I have been away from my home for far to long."

"Consider this your home now."

"That is very kind but I also promised my family and my father that I would return."

"…I see." His dissapointment did not shake his stance.

"Well I am sorry to hear that. But you know if there is anything that you would need in the future, you are always welcome to call me or Marcus." He leaned closer to Mohammed. "…But call me first."

"I will."

"Before I go let me give you your present." He reached into his pocket and pulled a silver packaged letter.

Mohammed opened it and saw that it was full of money and a deed to a piece of land. He pulled out the deed and noticed it was to an empty lot outside the Brooklyn borough.

"Oh this is too much Mr. Beacon. Really it is."

"Nonsense. Take it. You've earned it."

"I've hardly done that."

"Come now, it's a present."

"I can't take this, I haven't earned it."

"Of course you have."

"I've already made up my mind."

"You have? Then tell me. American Steel? Jared Brothers? Silver Firm? Who? I'll match it."

He was waiting to tell his mother and have her be the first to know. Mr. Beacon's sales pitch was digging into his skin.

"KDA."

"KDA?"

"Yes the Karachi Development Authority as a Master Planner."

"Karachi? There is nothing there for you."

"With all do respect Mr. Beacon, I think you of all people would implore a man to seek his own way."

"I would, but you have done so much more than that and only show a piece of paper for it. Karachi should owe you more than that."

"But that is what I have earned. I cannot really. I cannot." Mohammed handed him back the envelope just in time for Mrs. Beacon to observe. She came up behind Mohammed and pressed her hand against his shoulder.

"Now what are you two discussing this far away?"

"Just giving the boy his congratulations." Mr. Beacon replied for Mohammed.

"That's good. Yes. Congratulations."

"Darling we will be late for Marcus' ceremony at the hotel. Mohammed we will see you there right?"

Mohammed looked and smiled at both of them.

"Yes."

Behind them Marcus walked up and rolled his eyes, Mohammed contained his laughter.

"Good than we will see you there." Mr. Beacon pronounced.

Mohammed knew his next onslaught would be twice as daring and he would have the enlisted help of his peers. He had to get his rest before the next round. "Till then."

Marcus divided his two parents and embraced Mohammed. He whispered into his ear. "A few hours, don't leave me alone with them for that long. Be early." He turned around and the three made back to the car.

Mohammed watched them leave then made for his study hall. The vast hall was empty except for the receptionist sitting in the lobby. He walked next to her and signaled she went to the phone and prepared it for him.

He sat in a leather chair in next to the stone stairs leading to the first floor of the library. The receptionist connected to a host who migrated her to another. The connection was never very good; Mohammed often relied on letters to reach his family. He waited for a hint of optimism from the receptionist but there was nothing. The greatest day of his life he had to share it alone and he had to live it alone. Someone somewhere had to know of this. What good is an accomplishment if you cannot relish in it with someone else? He walked out of the hall and back to his room that was on the outskirts of the campus. It always relaxed him and gave him time to conjure ideas and plan out his thoughts. He would often stop midway and sit in the garden terrace stone courtyard outside his professor's office. It provided him with a welcome change of pace from the arrogant college students and lively crowd of buildings. It was this peace he would miss the most. He sat where he usually did and opened his degree to pull out the copy he had requested. This was the only was that he was sure his message of graduation would get to his mother, however difficult it would be for her. He put the rest of his papers away and continued to his room.

His room was stringent and musky. He had it all to himself for the past four years. His desk faced the door and created an office atmosphere so whenever someone entered it was strictly business. He kept all the letters from his family in the closet beneath his shoes. Pictures they sent were often ruined in transition but the few that did come out nicely he would proudly display above his window. After removing his cap and gown he sat in his desk and began writing a letter to his mother. Astonishingly it was only the third real letter he had ever sent her from college.

The others were full of pictures and small phrases like 'I love you' or 'see you soon' and 'get better soon.' He liked her to believe that he was too busy to write full letters. That he was too important to return a clear message. He kept her in his thoughts but it was not fair to his mother. She needed to see the prize he had just claimed. She had to live it with him and here of the pain and excitement it took for him to grasp it in his hands. All the emotions and all the time spent weaving conceptions and juggling ideas. She had to know it. She had to feel it.

He sat with a copy of his degree and pulled out a piece of paper and an envelope. The entire time he was making his way to his room he had planned out what he was going to write, but his mind could not afford him to create gibberish in order to fill a page. He sat for at least an hour thinking of what to write but the words didn't create themselves. His mother deserved better, his mother deserved humbling and modest words. Finally it came to him it was short and dull but at least it was something his mother would recognize. Putting pen to paper his idea was shockingly simple and would most likely be appreciated. He knew her condition stopped her from focusing on an idea for too long without getting a headache. It was obtuse and in poor taste. It was just words she was looking for. She needed some sort of familiarity to comfort her, while her mind was slowly decomposing. Although his letter would probably arrive in Pakistan around the time he would, it was still something she could hold on to. It was still something she could cherish and remember. Did it matter what the message was? Was she even conscious enough to get his letters? He wrote as legibly as he could. He stood up and left the words to dry and stain. He folded the copy of his degree and left the words in a shadow to conceive.

'Amma it is as you said, God forgives those who repent.' He enclosed it in the envelope along with his salvation.

10

Pakistan 1950

Karachi had changed over the course of the last few years. Much of that was to the success and pain of Mohammed. He had planned over half the new developments without any outside influence. His name was attached to several schools and libraries. This new project however was one that he could not afford to mess up. It was a mosque in dedication to his mother. It was only fair that it garnered her name. After all most of the schools and libraries took his father's name. Being a master planner was not as dubious as many had assumed, it required an extreme attention to detail and waiver of bribes, much of which had already been prescribed to his peers. They flaunted their desires to and from work, Mohammed was ashamed to call them his countrymen.

Karachi, it seemed grew as despairingly as Noor had. She had begun to lose her memories and sometimes her train of thought. Mohammed was sometimes a stranger or a hero when he arrived back at home. The servants kept her company and seemed to be more friend then subordinate to her. Some nights Mohammed would have to spend re-engaging his mother in his interests. Although she was not completely forgetful, Mohammed spent each night getting to know his mother in a new light. Stories of her childhood, her father, and day Ali died. She in turn would ask Mohammed for stories of work and America only after she was done talking, which usually didn't happen until she was exhausted. It was the same almost every night. Mohammed would guide her to her room and lay her on her bed, and listen to her weep from outside her bedroom door. However every morning she would wake up with Mohammed's degree frame in her embrace.

Mohammed was making his own way and was quite ready for marriage, he had been arranged many times before but none fit his desire. Many of the fathers that had introduced their daughters were more interested in Mohammed's title rather than his provided love. 'Master Planner for the KDA, what a infamous man.' He had often thought of what life would be like with the women he hardly knew. His father would approve of most any of them but his mother even in her condition would not, because none were good enough. He only knew of one young girl who would be an appropriate accommodation for him. She was barely finishing mid grade school and was of prime marriage age.

Mohammed's office building was one that belonged to the government, and one that Mohammed had built himself. It was far and away the most modern and technologically advanced thing Karachi had ever been a part of. Although it was only five stories tall he handpicked his office and team to follow. Unfortunately for Mohammed the rate in which they accepted bribes was far less than others he had considered.

The planning office was a mess; full of papers and blueprints, designing models and molding clay. He had foregone going home for the past two days while his peers went home to their families. On this night however he demanded his peers stay with him. He stood amongst them and had already gone over their proposals. Not one of them held a broad horizon for Karachi.

"What is this? What the hell is this junk?" He shouted at all of them. "This city doesn't need more malls or bazaars. And the mills that were proposed can be built outside the city for all I care! You were supposed to be reviewing government contracts, there is nothing stately about these abominations!"

"Mohammed" a shy voice from the front of the room sighed. "Karachi is full of development, why lose these proposals to the private contractors?"

"Because that is what they are paid for. They are running a business. We are running the state! It is very easy for you to lobby for them isn't it? A new car looks good in your driveway doesn't it Jamal? Or you Nasir? How about your daughters Saleem? They will be driven to success on the new horses on your farm!"

"What can you say Mohammed? Our mouths are bigger than our appetites!"

"What of Pakistan? How big is her appetite? This country is young and needs internal development, not commercial development. It has only been two years since her reception and you wish to pawn it off to these greed mongers."

"Pakistan will be supported by other countries. Let them bring the schools and libraries."

"Pakistan, gentlemen, is our duty to nurture. Who will bolster its flags and carry its knowledge beyond us? Your children and the spoon-fed hundred or the millions standing flat on their feet waiting for an opportunity! This country was not founded on your free trade demands. God gave it to us as a gift! By God! God doesn't live in malls or large home lots."

"They are only small bribes, they take more in a day in the parliament then we do in a year! And even so the other men in our very department barter their services for a hefty price."

"I will not have my name tarnished by your work. I will not allow it."

"We only ask for a small percentage."

Mohammed could see his message was not getting through to them. "Enough! If you ever bring me anything like this shit again I will have much more than your jobs, by Allah I will take something more dear and irreplaceable."

The few men in the room looked upon one another. Mohammed's message was ill advised but well met. The agreement came about from the pin drop silence after the bullying noise. The rest of the evening was spent balancing a budget after using it upon hand picked proposals. This was the time when Mohammed would create a meal ticket for the next decade and years beyond. He knew that his firm could handle only a few, but he made it a point to take on much more than his peers could handle. This was his way of taking their minds off of the attempted bribes that would continually arise. When the sun bristled above the shoreline horizon six new proposals had come about that were approved. Mohammed looked upon the beaten faces of his friends and decided to let them go unto their families. He would not hesitate for his family was crippled and dead.

He didn't know that his dreariness led him back to his office. The whole office was his- he could completely divulge ceiling tiles and shatter the windows. It wouldn't make a much of a difference and would create little interference. The office was empty and awaiting a lively freedom once Mohammed left. He could start a fire and saddle next to its warmth, or create a house of cards from filing cabinets. But nothing he held to this day would ever turn his attention from his work.

"Mohammed?" a delicate voice asked. "Mohammed, are you alright?"

He suspended his quest to look past the bounds in his office, and was deeply surprised by the figure in his presence. "Sophia?" He was shocked and flattered. She had evolved further into a beautiful woman. Her face was perfectly aligned with the rest of her body. She wasn't a lick older than twelve but looked as if she were scratching her late teens. The straight black hair that fell to her shoulders was pinned by jewelry and outlined her almond eyes. The nose piercing she wore was exactly as Mohammed had remembered it, a small golden flower that lay gently on her nose. Her elegance was overshadowed by her sheer commanding presence, most likely due to her splendor. She was a guiding light that gently entered his darkly created atmosphere. She pardoned the abhorrence in the office with each step she took. Even her walk was so elegant to Mohammed. She wasn't so much a force of infatuation as she was a welcomed innocence among his corrupted behavior.

"My father and mother are downstairs parking the car. They sent me up to give you this." It was a container of food concealed by six different compartments.

"Thank you? My how you've grown."

"Well when you don't see someone for many years that's any easy conclusion to come to."

"How is school?" The small talk was not what Mohammed had imagined when first talking to Sophia.

"It is good. How is work?"

"Work is a different set of pace, it's too much and too little at the same time." This was too much torture for Mohammed to take. He had thought about her for many, many days while working at the office. His curiosity did not do his passion justice.

"Your parents sent you in alone? Or did you wish to come up before they did?"

Sophia blushed and did not verbally respond. Instead she walked around his vicinity observing his wrecked office.

He stood barely alive waiting to reach out and touch her face. He had often thought of writing her or at least hearing her voice. But this moment had more than made up for his failures.

"My mother said it was because you needed some reminder of family." She remarked.

"Family?"

"Well I didn't quite say it like that." Sophia's mother emerged from the corner. "It was just my suggestion since you never come to see us and that you work so close."

Mohammed didn't obstruct his view from Sophia. He smiled at her hoping to catch a glimpse of a grin. It was more striking than he had ever imagined, even for a girl of her young age. It was something to behold.

"I am sorry that I have not made the time to visit with you. As you can see we are in over our heads here." He signaled for them to have a seat.

"We are only stopping for a short time. We really must be on our way. We have to be at you mothers house in a few minutes. But we expect to see you soon, right?"

"Yes, of course, as soon as I make time I will give it to you."

Sophia walked a few steps behind her mother out the door but not before turning back to smile at Mohammed. He returned her the favor and held his hand above his head to wave. He then silently worded to her: 'Thank you.' She blushed as she turned the corner. The day had once again reemerged from the drowsy emptiness.

Mohammed had a new proposal to think upon, perhaps his most important of all.

11

Pakistan 1950

Somber, silent, and wandering. Mohammed stared at his mother while she was sitting across the room reading a book of Nuwas' poetry. He wondered if she could even keep the thoughts about the intricate web of lyrics that was painted for her. Poetry was good for her. The lines were short and each was sweeter to the essence of Noor's soul than the last. The expressions on her face were like an infant trying to discover new meaning in the most mundane of things. Mohammed reached for the tea that was still steaming on a wheeled out cart.

"How is that one? Any different than the others?"

Noor briefly looked up from her book than focused once again on the words.

"They are all different."

"I don't know how you read that. It is far too complicated for me."

"We all have to try something difficult in our lives. Otherwise it wouldn't be much of a life, would it?"

Mohammed was pleased to see his mother had all her senses in tact tonight. He cautiously approached her with the tea he had just prepared for her. "Nuwas? What does he write about?"

"All things. Much of it was considered too… abstract… and irrelevant."

"Isn't that the way most poets are seen at first."

"Maybe, maybe not. Beauty from words comes from the sincerity and tenacity."

Mohammed was shocked to see the gradual transformation his mother had taken from being strictly religious to genuinely interested in new facets. Although she had not given up praying she was discovering new methods of meditation. "Maybe I should read that perhaps it could provide me with some inspiration."

"I don't think its inspiration you need." She commented while sipping her tea.

"Perhaps its peace than."

"No. I don't think it is that either. Everyone will soon be granted peace someday. Why work on something that you are already guaranteed?"

"Guaranteed? Where does it say that in the Quran?"

"I wasn't talking about the Quran."

Mohammed was sitting silently when his servant entered with message, which was handed to him. He opened the piece of paper and saw that it was from Sophia. He looked at his mother and saw that she immediately knew.

"Go." She unsmilingly wisped.

He felt abrupt. He knew he had to find her pardon before leaving. "Thank you." He said calmly then walked toward his study. He paused in the middle and turned back to see that his mother had put the book down and was stirring her tea. He walked back a little bit. "Amma, I have to take this." He signaled to the note. "I'm sorry." He walked back toward the study.

"For what, jaan?"

Mohammed stopped before opening the door to the study. His hand was on the handle. "Excuse me."

"Sorry for what, jaan?." She waited for a response. "What are you sorry for what?"

He stood holding onto the handle and didn't turn to look at her. He opened the door and escaped into the darkness. He closed himself off in the study. He didn't turn on the lights; he just put his forehead against the door and closed his eyes. It was not dark enough for him to find peace. It was just dark and empty. A familiar quiet void in which he had found himself far too often.

12

Pakistan 1950

The light created by the wedding tent was like a diamond sparkling in the sun. Lights shot off in all directions and brought in masses of guests to observe the next in line of several unions. The street walks were dabbled with red rose petals and magnolias were strung together and hung upon an entrance that separated like a curtain. The street was blocked off at both ends and only opened for preauthorized invitations. Security for the occasion was tightly broadcast to everyone. There were textile owners and commercial manufacturers that had been turned away several days in advance. This was not business, for the most part. A parade was cast down the street in honor of Mohammed and Sophia and extended into the distance.

Mohammed was arriving separately from his wife, on a white horse draped in flowers. Sophia was in the tent surrounded by other women who were pinning on lavish jewelry and putting together her extravagant red and gold wedding outfit. Mohammed had just come from a very successful meeting regarding the mosque he was set to build. Sophia was just taken from the playground she was playing on. His arrival was met with loud drums, applause, hugs and handshakes. Sophia's was met with tears. He was nervous and overly joyful. She felt the same way but could not show it around her mother and mother to be.

Inside the tent was a vast array of chairs and tables. Servants were secured at every entrance to make sure that every guest presented their invitation. Mohammed knew that people would become clever and try to mimic copies of his salutation. He was fully prepared to turn away anyone he did not know or anyone he didn't care for.

The fires used to prepare the food for the guests created smoke from behind the tent.

Even though the invitations had stated an arrival time of five Mohammed and his bride to be knew that the guests would pay no attention to detail. Mohammed was strict on time. He instructed his servants to turn away anyone who did not show up before five thirty. He would not have anyone ruin his most anticipated day to build his life. He carried the same sense of urgency in all walks of his life. Karachi needed a strict rule to live by; he was only the budding microcasm that it would try to build from.

Sophia could hear her husband-to-be beyond the silk covered walls. His intensity was something that Sophia admired. With every deep resounding echo in his voice the women around Sophia would giggle and smile at her. She knew that Mohammed was a very rare commodity to the families in Pakistan. Many fathers and mothers wanted him as a son and many girls wanted him as a provider. She looked at herself almost ready in the mirror. The red gown bled from head to toe. It was outlined with gold frills and gold jewelry that was sprinkled on her face. Her nails were painted beyond the hands and feet that were designed with henna. She imagined herself no longer in school with her friends but next to her husband. That would be her life from now on. She took pride in the fact that she was the first of her friends and family her age to get married.

Mohammed anxiously waited for the ceremony to begin. He looked upon the crowd that was gathering below. His mother was near the entrance in her wheelchair wordlessly accepting people into the tented hall. His family and friends did not approach Mohammed on the elevated stage yet. Children Sophia's age were running around skirting under tables. They were all waiting for the marriage to be completed before approaching and congratulating. His co-workers from the office entered clearly better dressed than most of the crowd.

Jamal, one of his bold peers, had spotted Mohammed and uninvitingly approached him. He stuck out his hands and went for a hug. He embraced Mohammed tightly while pronouncing his soon-to-be wife's name to him. "Sophia Ahmed. Mubarak." He drew back while holding on to Mohammed's shoulder's "I have a present for you." He signaled to his servant that brought forth a suitcase.

"Not now Jamal there is a table for that." Mohammed looked on to the crowd embarrassed.

"No its very important you look at this."

"Can't it wait."

"No its very important. Lets just say it's from 'my family.' He winked at Mohammed.

The servant walked up the two stairs to the stage where Mohammed sat. It was decorated with a sofa and two chairs, adorned with pillows, silk curtains, roman columns lights, flowers. He cracked open the suitcase. It was full of rupees and from what Mohammed could see a rolled up blueprint. Mohammed's heart started to pound. Every ounce of decency in his body controlled him from attacking Jamal. Instead he calmly closed the suitcase and signaled for Jamal to follow him to the back of the tent. Jamal took hold of the suitcase. His servant dispersed into the crowd.

Mohammed's hands were clinching over and over again. He gritted his teeth and stretched his neck. Outside the tent servants were shuffling back and forth making fresh naan and preparing moist kabobs and uncapping several soda bottles. When Jamal made his way out following Mohammed, he was grabbed by the neck and thrown against the wall.

"My wedding Jamal, I told you I want no part in this, and you bring this to my wedding! I am not nor will I ever be for sale!"

Jamal knew in the back of his head he might have to deal with such a reaction. He didn't react quite as Mohammed planned. Instead he laughingly proclaimed. "Not for sale Mohammed? You are sucking the life out of Pakistan. You make more than all Saleem, Nasir, and I make. And you snicker at us for wanting a life such as yours."

"My life is not yours to barter!" He pressed harder with his hands he could feel the air thinning from Jamal's lungs. The servants had suspended their duties to watch without coming to Jamal's aid. Mohammed looked at them. "Get on with it."

The servants stumbled back to their tasks.

Mohammed let go of his neck. Jamal fell to his knees gasping for air. "You… don't even know… who it is from."

"Even if it were from my father or God himself, it has no place here… And neither do you. I warned you Jamal, I warned you what would happen if you brought this upon me." He grabbed Jamal by the hands and helped him to his feet.

He was a little dizzy but for some reason not shocked. "It is not from a commercial site or mall it is for a mosque."

Mohammed sarcastically replied. "A mosque?"

"Your mosque. The one you planned. The Suddiqqi Firm proposed a new plan for it."

Mohammed took the briefcase that was lying on the floor and opened it. He reached for the blueprints tucked in the back. Opening it he could see that it was a map and site planned for Tariq road. He bowed his head down in disappointment. "If there is one thing I can teach you Jamal it is this." He drew his finger down the road toward the planned site. "Look at the size of the mosque Jamal."

Jamal peered closer. "It is large and only planned for a mosque. So?"

"It is seven floors? Look at the buildings surrounding this area they are all flats." He pointed out several other lots in the area. "What mosque have you ever been in that had seven floors Jamal?"

Jamal's facial expression told Mohammed his point had reached its destination. Mohammed rolled up the blueprints and put them back in the suitcase and locked it. He handed it to Jamal "Anything that sounds to good to be true usually is, Jamal." He patted him on the back "Karachi is structurally unsound. Greed exists everywhere. Do not make the mistake of underestimating our country. It may be young but it is still clever."

Jamal straightened up and looked at Mohammed he turned in the direction of tent and made his way back in. Mohammed stopped him from continuing. "No Jamal I cannot have you back in there." He signaled for him to leave out the back way, through the servant's preparation area.

Jamal was appalled. "Mohammed it is over. I apologize."

"You should know better Jamal. I'm sorry old friend. I cannot have you here. I don't want to feel embarrassed, so leave this way."

Jamal knew once Mohammed had made up his mind that it was impossible to change. He walked out the back a defeated man.

Mohammed watched and waited for him to completely wane. The night was just beginning but this wasn't the way Mohammed had imagined it to start. He looked at the time, it was getting late, too late for Mohammed's liking. The hall was almost full and the ceremony was waiting on Mohammed's word to begin. He made it back to the slightly elevated stage where an Imam was sitting on the decorated couch snacking on the sweets left for the bride and groom. His tri-colored beard spread out from his entire face, it started black faded to white then red.

Mohammed disliked him and his sense of self-importance, but he was a respected man and Sophia's family requested his services. Mohammed stood and cast his shadow down on his guests from above.

A servant appeared from the back of the tent and signaled to Mohammed to begin the service. Mohammed's heart jumped into his throat and began beating quicker and quicker as he signaled back. A few seconds passed as a parade of Sophia's family entered the hall. A canopy made from a silk cloth hovered above Sophia's head. Mohammed could not completely see her. He waited as the procession snaked its way to the front of the hall and onto the stage. He was hoping that Sophia shared his anxiety; he cared more to see her face, for it had been several days since they had gazed upon each other. The Imam's coughing and clearing his throat of flem continually interrupted the atmosphere. Sophia's float drew near and Mohammed now had a clear view of his elegant bride. He wanted to reach his hand out and pull her up next to him. He had to wait until they were officially announced husband and wife. The Imam sat on the couch, Mohammed sat on his left and Sophia was sat down on his right. The procession of most her family dispersed into the hall, while most the men in her family stayed on the stage to witness the signing of the marriage certificate. The Imam thoroughly read through the document to make sure both names were always spelled correctly. He looked at Mohammed and asked him to sign, and then did the same to Sophia. He joined their hands to a slight applause on the stage, which was quickly dismissed by the Imam.

The Imam began reciting a prayer that faded in the gaze shared between Mohammed and Sophia.

He was hers and she was his. Their eyes did not flinch nor share a hint of mistrust.

Instead they had taken each other to a safe and humble place hidden in each other's hearts and minds. The softness of her hands equally balanced out the calluses on his. The longest, darkest moments in his life eased away. The future was just beginning for Sophia, but she was in a safe embrace that young girls would only often dream about. Both had thought of this day as being one that had to pass but not one that they wanted to pass. A sweet music arose from the grasp she placed in Mohammed's hands. It was cast into his body and exuded through his ears. She would gently squeeze his hand and see how Mohammed would respond. The redness that colored out his face almost matched her ensemble. Her lips were perfectly curved and her skin was more smooth and gentle than anything that he had known, or wanted to know. The world did not stop nor even slow down. Instead the pace at which it existed was exactly as it had come about. In her he sought calmness, and in him was a shred of doubt in the world that she needed to experience. No words were spoken between the two while the Imam sat between them. All they had to know and all they had to say came about in that particular moment.

"You are now husband and wife." The Imam interrupted. As he rose between the two he took another sweet that was intended for the two.

Sophia reached into the box and broke off a piece of sweetened dough. She brought it to Mohammed's mouth and fed it to him as he did the same for her. They both were so caught in the moment they didn't notice the flashes of cameras and mumble of the crowd. There was no one between them now, only around them.

"Mubarak!" a man had come and shook Mohammed back to reality.

Mohammed confusingly asked himself Mubarak? He realized where he was and how he had to receive the crowd one person at a time. He looked at the figure that stood before him. It was Sophia's father who started a line of congratulations that bended to the entry of the tent. He stood to accept the congratulations with his wife's hand in his.

No longer did he have to accept anything alone. Everything he did from this moment on he would do with her in mind. Mohammed and Sophia embraced her father and then her mother. They were led to Mohammed's mother who was sitting looking at the ground.

"Salaam amma jaan." Sophia spoke while holding both her hands looking for her to make contact.

"Oh Sophia. My how you've grown." She commented.

Sophia looked up at Mohammed who slightly nodded. He then bent down to accept her unknowing blessing.

"Mubarak amma." He commented.

"Mubarak? For what my boy?" she looked around to the crowd.

Mohammed took hold of his wife before she went to explain. He shook his head and they stood their observing her observing the two of them. The moment was not as either of them had pictured it. But it was theirs and that's all they could live by.

Mohammed wanted very much for his mother to acknowledge this as something beyond her eyes. The two didn't want to spend too much time ignoring the scene around them. They had their lives beyond this time to live with Mohammed's mother and try to resolve what couldn't be. It tore Mohammed up to know that she couldn't know more about this union. Just as many things before this, something else would tear Mohammed from his mother.

They made their rounds about the hall and visited with each family designated at each table. They were greeted with the same effect each time, usually a 'Mubarak' and an envelope or boxed gift. The most awkward part of their journey through the maze of tables and servants came at the greeting of Sophia's friends. They were focused on playing and slapping hands, while she crossed the line over to adulthood before they had. They all marveled and poked at her dress while she managed to keep a straight face. It was one of the reasons Mohammed had found her to be extraordinary. She held a maturity that was foreign to some women even twice her age.

Women and men alike thought it was a good match, he would bring her everything and take her anywhere, while she would do the same thing. They went back to the stage where a table for two was created. They were so anxious and excited that they did not even eat when food was brought to their table. Instead they looked around and lived in the instances that were specifically created for them.

The night was a mixture of a slowed mood mixed with quickly a forgotten quaintnence. Mohammed was ready to whisk his bride and officially make her his.

The march out to the waiting limousine was perhaps the longest part of the evening. Every family member and close friend waited in row to receive the two as they left the hall. A Quran was placed above Sophia's head as she passed through the horde. Mohammed's side greeted the two with cheers and smiles, while Sophia's side drowned the two with tears. The limousine was decorated with white rose petals to match. The noise came to a halt once the door shut and the two sighed to each other.

"Are you happy?" Mohammed immediately asked.

She didn't know how to respond for she knew her happiness would grow with each passing moment with him. "Time will tell."

The ride to the hotel was filled with laughter and surprise of new facts learned about each other. The limousine drove past the roadblock and toward the hotel. Both of them were nervous and didn't want it to stop- at least not yet. The reality of marriage slowly hit them as they were finally alone.

The fact was as simple as the difference in their age. As much as they loved each other they were still strangers.

13

Pakistan 1953

The room was cold and dark. Light had not been let in for a long time. Boxes had been piled up in the corner ready to be unearthed once again. Dust had gathered on most everything. The bed had a crease created in it from overexposed to a body. It was the one room in the house that was rarely visited, or entered. Other than its usual tenant who had since passed it was an exotic world that existed to Mohammed and Sophia inside their home.

"What of this one Mohammed?" Sophia asked as she pulled boxes from the closet.

"No don't bend down, I'll get that." Mohammed rushed to her aid and straightened her out. He then pressed his hand against her stomach. "You don't need to stress, especially while you are pregnant."

The boxes that were being emptied belonged to Mohammed's since passed mother. Her passing came around Sophia and Mohammed's second anniversary.

"Why don't you go and rest on the bed, I will have the servants prepare you something of comfort." Mohammed tried appealing to her better nature.

"I am alright. I would very much like to help you clean out this area." She responded.

"It's going to take more than one day. There will be other days to help." He shot back.

"I know that you want to do this alone. But I am always here for help. You forget she was my family as well."

Mohammed could see that she wasn't going to budge. "At least sit in that chair. I will bring you boxes to clear." He sifted through light boxes and placed them at Sophia's feet. "Just the documents, nothing more."

"What of pictures and--"

"No just documents, that is all I am interested in right now."

Mohammed returned to his corner and went through the boxes as before. It was work that he was not accustomed to. However he couldn't trust his servants to go through these materials, they would end up stacking on his desk because of their illiteracy. He went to the window and opened the curtains. The light had revealed an even sadder scene than what had originally been thought.

"This room has not seen light in quite some time."

"My mother liked the dark for some reason. I believe it brought her peace she could not have."

"I always thought that your mother never trusted anyone, that's why the door was always locked and the curtains always drawn."

"Perhaps that is how we shall become in our elder years. Life has a mystery that only unravels with time. The only things she could trust were the things she held governance over."

Sophia opened the box next to her and dove in. Mohammed gathered the ones around him and followed suit. He was driven into the past with photo's of his father standing in his prime looking over a project. There were things that didn't seem to belong and items that would evoke a deep resentment, but it was not Mohammed's time to reflect on anything except his parentless life. This was the first time that Mohammed had echoed into his past without looking for help. He looked over his shoulder and saw that Sophia had already made a pile of documents and refuge. Mohammed was looking for certain aspects and things he did not want his wife to see.

Time would pass as easily as the boxes were separated and flattened. The room started to become familiar once again. Mohammed built the house a few weeks before he got married. His mother had occupied this room that was originally designed for their first child. Although there were several rooms in the house left this was the ideal location for a first child. Mohammed didn't question when his mother requested this room, but time was an asset that only he and Sophia had. The room was going to be emptied and redone to properly accommodate a nursery.

"Tell me again what color you want this room to be painted?" Mohammed rhetorically asked.

"White with a purple outline."

Mohammed shuffled through papers while continuing his focus on Sophia. "What if it is a boy?"

"That's why I chose white."

"So you are playing both sides? Or do you know?"

"Just covering both grounds." She answered with a smirk.

"You know we never really talked about names."

"What do you like?"

"Anything that you choose as long as its not Munira or Shamiana."

"Those were my top two choices."

"Really now, you haven't even given me a hint."

She smiled "Oh you want a hint okay it starts with an S and ends with and A." She began to laugh harder as she saw that her joke had hit home. Even he couldn't contain himself.

The light in the room only enhanced the drowned darkness that was becoming evident. Light wasn't just shut out it was purposely kept out, to preserve and to keep hidden the secrets in the room. It was the only place in the enormous house in which Mohammed and Sophia were not allowed to enter without strict permission. The bedroom was like the others but this one was twisted, and broken.

"What should I do with this?" Sophia asked as she tossed an enclosed folder to Mohammed's back.

"Let me see." He opened it and sifted through the papers. It was written in an older form of calligraphy not used today with modern adjustments made to everything. He immediately noticed his name and began looking for anything else of use. There it was as clear and as forgotten as the room had made it. Ravinder Patel. The name sharpened Mohammed's senses and brought him back to a world he had sought to forget. All his work, all his study had led him back around to this point. He read the paper from top to bottom. It was never clearly justified to him how his life was spared, or how his father was able to spare it. As many things in his childhood, if it was not taken care of by his father already then it was of no use to continue to ponder upon. It was as clear and simple as a clean pardon only someone's blood had to be spilt in order for a blood right to be exonerated. Mohammed's name was stated upon a blood right removal…Blood Rights. It was a phrase that had died with the westernization of the Indian sub-continent. It was the reason he was able to become the man he was today. Blood Rights. An eye for and eye, or at least in his case with Ehsan, harm upon harm. His father had signed this and so had Ravinder, so that Mohammed or his father never had to live in fear. His life was spared and then hidden away in a dusty dim room. However, neither Ravinder, Ehsan or Ali had died that night. There was no explanation of the miracle his father was able to create. It was never mentioned, merely forgotten. This room held secrets that had awakened with a death. Mohammed read on. His father had sold all the rights of the land that his neighbors had lived on. Mohammed's life was worth more than a rich landowner, his son, and half the district block that lived with him. The dying caste was in its infantile state. Someone had to have been martyred for Mohammed's life to continue, but who? He kept thinking to himself what life was worth his own. Then the name came flying out of his mouth strangely involuntarily. "Abdullah." A sacrifice from both families.

"Abdullah?" Sophia questioned.

"…Oh…He was a servant of ours."

"Do those things belong to him?"

Mohammed stayed silent. 'They should' he thought to himself. It never became clear to him how his blood was spared. Someone's blood had to be spilt in a manner that benefited both Blood Right parties. "Abdullah."

"Do you miss him that much?"

Mohammed had never given a thought to why Abdullah was never talked about again. He was as much a ghost as he was when he was a servant.

"Do we need to keep that?" Sophia questioned.

"Umm. Well… No. Not at all." He grabbed another piece of paper and acted as he was crumpling it. He slipped the pardon into a pile that he was keeping.

"Good. I was about to throw it away."

"Oh. Good." He was still focused on his father and the secrets he died with. His mother had kept this secret since the time that they were fleeing to Karachi. His mother was very good at deflecting his inquiry, perhaps his fathers greatest feet was compelling Mohammed to believe Ravinder was a myth and that Abdullah was really a pawn. The fact still loomed with Mohammed that no longer did he understand his father nor want to. That day in the hotel room, those noises and screams belonged to a woman who understood the death wish Mohammed's father had signed. He recollected the memories of the paper he saw in through the cross twined sack, and how easily those words of land separation jumped into his mind. How easy it was to spill blood. Mohammed was in disbelief and clarity at the same time. Whether he would hold the truth to be self-evident or shut it away as was tradition, the fact was as clear as he had ever thought it to be. His father condemned and betrayed Abdullah for the sake of Mohammed's pride. No matter how Mohammed spun the truth his father was held in new regards.

14

"Abu, Abu when are you coming home?" The tiny voices over the phone tickled Mohammed's heart.

"Shehla, Neeloofer. I want to see your reading progress when I get home." Mohammed replied.

"Okay Baba."

"Put your mother on the phone." He heard giggles on the other side of the line. Then the phone went silent. As much as she needed to speak with her, his anger would never retreat toward his daughters. And rarely did it find its way to his once again pregnant wife. His only outlet was his work.

The days were longer and the time spent away from his family was not what he imagined. The Abdullah Mosque he had planned was nearing completion. It was the remaining project he had taken on nearly ten years ago. This project was refreshing; he rarely had to push away bribes in order to complete it. His stance on the corruption he faced had become synonymous with the ferocity he conveyed toward easily bribed peers. The solace he felt at work was now only felt home, where his family surrounded him. He had to continually surround himself with pictures and homey touches in order to keep his sanity. A picture of his wife, his oldest daughter as and infant, and himself holding her was in the middle of his desk. His peers would look into his office with an odd look on their faces. The extravagant ambiance created in their offices made Mohammed's humbleness look cowardly. He didn't mind how odd it made him look, rather he cared how corrupt it made his office look.

He could no longer hold back how much money his peers accepted, rather put a cap on how much they would take. His co-workers would show up with larger cars, pricier suits, and more servants. He nurtured them. Then they all turned on him and diffused into other parts of the government firm where they weren't constantly criticized. Even though he controlled the planning that was done, his peers got smart and creative. They would funnel the bribes through other channels in the firm. The only thing Mohammed could do was focus on his work, it was the one thing he could control without corruption. He would seldom use his old peers for projects he was working on. When he did use them it would be with small outlets in which the bribes were funneled in with smaller amounts. It was important to engulf himself in a world that had no corruption. Shehla, Neeloofer, and his wife helped with that.

A knock on his doorframe broke his concentration. It was Jamal, who had a guest with him.

"Yes Jamal. What is it?"

He entered and was followed by a large hefty gentleman. He wore a traditional Punjabi hat and a three-piece grey suit. His walk assumed him to be an important man. His shaved face with pencil thin mustache took the attention away from his thick eyebrows and intense stare. A gold chain disappeared into his suit vest. No doubt God's name was hanging from the end of it. His face had many miles treaded upon it and from the way he positioned his hat Mohammed could tell he was halfway bald. He was infamous before Mohammed knew his name.

"I would like you to meet Faraz Ibrahim." Jamal introduced.

The man waited for Mohammed to rise and greet him. Mohammed knew what this meeting was about the second he entered his door. Mohammed did not get up, instead he presented his hand from across his desk. The man looked at Jamal with a questioning face, then back at Mohammed. He came to his hand and shook it and sat without being invited. Faraz then signaled to Jamal to leave, he did so without hesitation.

"Mohammed Ahmed, your name travels farther than Pakistan can reach." His flattery was practiced.

"Mr. Ibrahim." Mohammed calmly replied while nodding.

"Am I interrupting something?"

"I am always interrupted. Your interruption just happens to be casual."

Faraz looked upon Mohammed's desk and reached for the picture frames. "What a beautiful family. Would you like to see a picture of my family?" Without a word of agreement from Mohammed, Faraz reached into his pocket and pulled out his wallet. He handed him a picture of an entire cast of millworkers stationed outside a mill and posing for a camera. They were holding shovels and aprons. Many of the faces did not carry any sort of life in them, just patches of dirt or smudges of color. A few were smiling, but Mohammed could sense it wasn't for the right reasons.

"What a large family you have."

"That is what everyone says. Although I know you that you know better than that."

He held up Mohammed's picture after grabbing it from Mohammed. "This is what a family should look like." He held up his wallet-sized picture. "Not this."

His approach was awkward, but it had engaged Mohammed's interest. Any person who took an immediate interest in his family was at least worth hearing out.

Upon seeing his method was working Faraz popped open his briefcase. "It is important for families to have health. Health can come from any outlet, food, education, family, even clothing. I am not a businessman. I would like to think of myself as someone who caters to the needs of families. Since you have a family perhaps this would be a good outlet for you to ponder upon? We all have our fancies in this life. I know that you are constantly pressured with proposals that do not suit you or Karachi."

For the first time Mohammed had a feeling that a person with some knowledge of his astute ways was encouraging him. He sat impatiently waiting for Faraz to finish his speech and present him with a plan that could be used to help further Karachi. He kept talking but Mohammed tuned out. In his business dealings Mohammed learned to catch only a few words that his counterpart would offer. Instead he would use that time to uncover their hidden agenda by looking through their words and upon their actions. Faraz kept eye contact, he didn't make lame attempt with humor or gestures. He always stood upright and had an agenda the whole time. It was difficult for Mohammed to expose.

"We all have a place in this world, Mr. Ahmed. I would like very much to create one for our children to prosper in." He handed him an envelope. "Please do not open this yet. I would like you to take a drive to this location." He pointed to the intersection on a map that was taped to the envelope. "Then when you are there look around to see the condition children live in, then look at this plot and see what I have proposed. I believe Allah will guide you to do the right thing."

Faraz had a way of forbidding the future. His encouragement only intrigued Mohammed, with an outlined sense of disappointment. There was a tension in the room when Faraz got up to leave, but it wasn't one that caused harm. Mohammed stood up with him and preceded him to the door.

"Please remember not to open the envelope until you get to the site." Faraz said as his last words. He walked to the door at the end of the hall and down the stairs.

Mohammed was a taken back by the way he did not present himself. Even for the men that would come to bribe him he would present himself and stand up. This time he just stayed in his seat and listened without disruption. The envelope was alone in his office beckoning to Mohammed to be opened. It was an interesting thought to see what it was that Faraz had suggested. The envelope waited and waited and waited some more. Mohammed started to tap the desk without a steady beat with his finger. He lost his concentration on his prior work. The prospect of discovering a new development first hand was enough motivation. He came back to reality and picked up the phone next to him.

"Hello?" Sophia answered on the other line.

"Jaan, it's me. I am going to be late tonight. Don't wait for me to eat."

"But the girls are waiting for you." Sophia said disappointed.

"I will still be there, just belated is all. I have to go so that I can try to make it back somewhat on time."

Sophia hung up and didn't ask questions, she knew better than to interfere in matters she was not educated in.

Mohammed hung up and gathered his things. He didn't notice Jamal at the end of the hall spying on him. Mohammed had the uncanny ability to remove wandering and intense eyes off of him, even if he didn't know he was being watched.

It was a good sign to Jamal that Faraz was able to get him to go. Perchance this was the beginning of something new for Mohammed, and something better for Jamal.

Mohammed checked his watch and completed shutting down his office. It was a routine that he was fairly accustomed. He had his office secured more tightly than any other office in the building, and probably the city. His cabinets had three locks on each opening while his desk was custom fitted with two safes guarded below the drawers. The only thing left unsafe were the pictures of his family scattered throughout his office.

He looked to see the suns position for the next time for prayer. The rush home had not yet started and if he could get his driver to hurry he wouldn't be caught in the absurd amount of traffic. He locked the door to his office and went downstairs to the entrance. He didn't bother saying goodbye to anyone, or even making eye contact, his feet scuttled hastily for the door, as if he were trying to catch a taxi. A lobby boy was squatting on the floor and counting his money that was strewn on the floor. He became aware of Mohammed after Mohammed forcefully cleared his throat. The boy didn't even look up he just cleaned up his small amount of money and went in search of Mohammed's driver. The car careened around the corner a few minutes later. Mohammed seated himself in the back and waited to give the instruction of direction to his driver.

His moment of sputtering readiness was now of calm collectiveness. There was something about the presentation from earlier that he wanted to go over. Something that he couldn't grasp, or maybe it was something he needed to understand more. It was the way it was presented that he had to know. The mystery of discovery was intensely pulling him to a reality. He was now able to share in the idea of his peers without indulging in their guilt.

The driver did not say a word and waited for Mohammed to motion. It was a life that he had lived for many years. Patience was his greatest attribute, and while he was paid handsomely he was never trusted with anything. He rarely drove any place alone with the car. Mohammed's daughters were more preciously observed than his work. The only case of freedom he had was creating a route to the destination that was chosen.

"I need you to take me here." Mohammed leaned forward and showed the driver the intersection taped on the envelope.

"Yes sahib." The driver responded as he shifted the car into gear, and did the only thing he was appreciated for, driving.

Mohammed watched the scenery unfold outside the safety of his tinted glass. This was a route that he would usually take to his in-laws home, it was the first time he was using it for business. The scene began to change from office buildings and mosques, to dirt roads and barren scrublands back to buildings outlined with cement blocks stacked upon one another turned into homes. The sea of brown colored lots and wall protected homes turned to colorfully displayed advertisements and endlessly stretching buildings. Mohammed could hardly believe that this was the main road used by Karachi. It started at the sea and spread inward. He usually traveled this road at night; it was alien in the daylight.

The street, which Mohammed came to, was strum with uneven gutters and loud signs that cast musical and movie stars onto the unworthy crowd below. Like a light cast from the heavens the corner which Mohammed was observing was the only one that was illuminated by the sun. Cattle, donkeys, cars, and light bikes ran the streets and faded in and out of the fragments of light that were dissected by the surrounding buildings. From two lanes of designated road came eight lanes of created traffic. This was the farthest Tariq road had ever taken him. It was the closest thing to Pakistan that he had seen in a while. The driver pulled to the right and gave Mohammed a clear view of the street corner. Without hesitation Mohammed knew which corner Faraz wanted to choose for his project. It was on the Southwest side, the building was darkened, and only to be illuminated from within by lights brought in by squatters. It was crumbling to the floor creating a mess of stones on the road. It looked more like a mound of scattered gray piles than it did a completed project. Children were running freely in the streets, some clothed, and some naked. Mother's held their infants close to their breasts while tugging on the pant legs of people passing by. Cracks in the street were filled with wooden planks that barely held steady over passing cars. Clothes were cast off of drying lines spread from home to home across streets. Children attacked cars that stopped in their vicinity, and banged on the windows crying and asking for money. This was the Karachi Mohammed wanted to fix. It was the one that a majority of Pakistani's lived in. No matter how far Mohammed fared from it, with his work and home, this was behind every business decision he made.

His car gained notoriety from the children as soon as it was spotted. They surrounded it and began to cry and present it with their torn off limbs and jagged scars. Mohammed was not immune to their bellows. He handed the driver some money and told him to spread it amongst the children; the driver did so without delay. They snatched it from his hands like a fish does bait off of a hook. They swarmed around the tallest child who gathered all the money. Mohammed watched as the child gathered the money and struggled to count it, he gave up half way and they went on to the next scrum waiting. They were extremely street smart, their craft was shaped by their clever tongues and saddened façade. The children capitalized where the elder woman and men could not.

People nowadays were more inclined to help a child rather than a mother or father. These men and women resorted to things the children had not yet been exposed. They resorted to drugs and cutting themselves as a manner to relieve the stress and pain.

Before opening the envelope he observed the poor like animals wandering on the street. They had no place they belonged to or place they could be safe. The street was an education that taught them the ways to barely survive. It was this scrappy method that Mohammed sought to rid Karachi of, and in turn Pakistan. A school or library at every corner was more important than a market or pharmacy.

Every child gets sick, but not every child has the means to take themselves out of a poverty stricken life.

The noise left with the children down a block. The day turned slowly into night. The call to prayer was sounded above the buildings. The streets emptied and filled into the mausoleum styled mosque adjacent to the corner Mohammed had come to see. Now was the time that Mohammed had anticipated he would open the envelope. He held it in his hands and looked at the seal. It was taped, glued and fastened to the command of Faraz's mysterious ways. He cut it open with his fingers and pulled the packet from within. He wanted very much for this proposal to work. His heart could barely take another disappointment. He opened it and his fears were confirmed. It was a proposal set up for a textile mill. As he read the proposal he crumpled the envelope in his hands. He knew he would have to eventually come to this type of conclusion. There was a need for cheap labor, labor that families would fill with their children.

It was the hardest thing that he had already thought of for many drawn out days. He didn't know how to come to any sort of conclusion. His life just mandated that he choose the lesser of two evils. On the one hand this would take children off the street and give them the life that Mohammed wanted to see them in. On the other if the mill was built it would take these children out of any sort of education equation. He looked at the empty street and imagined a mill feeding the industry in this area. He could also see a school on the corner; an empty squatter school that sold seldom-used smarts to these same children. It would not change the fact that the parents of the children would either force them into labor, or from school. Mohammed wanted very much to ignore this and have it go away. It was this type of decision that he had to make now.

He looked again and saw the mill fashioned above the surrounding complexes. He saw smoke billowing from the pillars and the men rushing back and forth between the mill and the mosque. The area had turned from shanty into commercial nightmare. Children were born solely to bring money back to their families. While it was a better life for Mohammed to imagine for these children it wasn't the way he pictured any child to grow in his Pakistan.

He sifted through the proposal while rubbing his forehead. He knew that if he didn't open the sight to the mill, the department down the hall would do it for a higher cost. His mind was set upon stopping the harm before it began. He took out a notepad hidden away in his briefcase and jotted notes about the area. He started with the broken street and began to fix the busted homes and shops in his mind. Finally his attention transferred to the broken building. He was now recreating an area that had no proposal set for what he had in mind. Tariq road was becoming the Karachi that Mohammed had planned. It was different but it needed to happen. The sporadic involvement of different projects was taking Karachi nowhere. Even though several things were created with the best intentions, together they were far apart, and in no way able to create a change.

With the new project in mind, Mohammed had taken the proposal given to him by Faraz and began ripping it page by page. It was dangerous, and he did not want his peers to consider it. If this type of industry were brought into this part of Tariq road, there would be no stopping its conquest to the sea. With each rip he saw his vision coming to life. He wanted to see a Pakistan that was united in developing an interest in all her children. He was as giddy as the children that had come to collect money from him. He saw the end of the bribes and the beginning of a new era living its life in the streets of Karachi, beginning with Tariq road. He ripped and tore each page creating a pile of shredded millwork on the floor. He sealed his fate and that of Pakistan's with each tare. He didn't care anymore. No longer would there be a system of caste in his city. No longer would a child have to choose between a book or a time card. His city would live to the promise his father sought after and it would begin with his blood, sweat, and tears. Faraz was the last suitor to come seeking a marriage. He came to the final paper and looked at the picture that was a blown up version of the one Faraz had shown him in his office. He now saw that these were children that grew with the mill. With closed eyes and ears he ripped it into several pieces and snowed it upon the car floor. He was clean of it, and it would not have a hold on him any longer. Faraz had led him to the final conclusion, the way no one had before. Mohammed's fate and Karachi's future walked hand in hand, he looked out the window and hoped that it would be begin down this street. Mohammed straightened himself after kicking the papers around, he reached into his pocket and looked at the driver.

"How much did I give those children?"

15

Mohammed looked up at the hypnotizing stairwell. He was dizzy just looking at it. He had to close his eyes to balance the effect of what he thought was vertigo. Mohammed stepped up onto the first step and began his conquest of each floor. The only thing that brought him comfort was focusing on each step taken to ascend. Seven floors was never a task that he couldn't handle. But he was winded after the first floor. 'I must be tired' he told himself. He had to stop and regain his breath. His heart was pounding at a rate that was not recognizable. 'It must be the tea.' He spent the next minute trying to take his mind off of the daunting task of climbing the stairs. He had to remind himself of the reason he would take the stairs. It was the place in which he would find a peace that echoed with each moment he rose. Elevator's were quick and provided lies about the buildings they were in. You can lie about a stairwell. It comes with hidden details that many architects are too proud to fix. Each crack, each nook, and each beam had a different story to tell Mohammed. This was a way that he would travel. He would never request to stay on a floor higher than the tenth floor that way he could stay humbled even in the most luxurious atmosphere. It annoyed his wife, she would always wait and wait for him to make it to the top while he was taking the stairs. He reached the third floor and had to take a seat.

"Not even half way." His mother's voice sounded in his mind.

He had to be hallucinating the voice was as clear as if it were seated next to him.

It did not echo as it would have, had it been said in the stairwell, rather it clearly entered and exited his ears.

The concentration he put upon himself to get up was something that he would

only uncover for his work. Once his breath was back with him, he took it with him to the next floors. The top was falling down on him in a repetitive circular motion. He began to lose focus on the stairs and focus more on each stair he would have to take. He could feel the blood coursing through his veins. It rushed through his heart and gathered in the midst of his head. The world around him began to rumble in his eyes. His determination would not take him any further. His left eye was twitching and pumping the same beat of his heart.

Fifth floor.

There was no way that Mohammed could continue this stress. He exited on this floor and rested in the lighter area near the elevator. He walked to the window to try and clear his head. The pain was astounding in his head. He could not rid himself of it. He had to try and avoid the pain. The lights of homes in the distance dotted around every corner of the window. They were like fireflies scattering in the cool night. Perhaps it was the calm vibe of a new city or the excruciating sting in his forehead that caused him to prop himself again the window. He looked straight down the side of the hotel. A flashing light in the corner of his eye brought his view to the gated entrance of the hotel. Two cars had piled against one another and blocked the entrance. Policemen and paramedics worked like rodents to clear the fire that broke out amongst the cars. The fire built and stopped any of the workers from stepping foot on hotel grounds.

"I must be hallucinating." Mohammed said with head pressed against the window. His words created a fog that mucked the screen. He wiped it away and only to see the fire raging harder and harder. Men from inside the hotel ran to the fire and tried to douse it from their side. Mohammed had barely noticed the small crowd gathering around him. He could see that this was the most exciting thing they had seen in quite some time from the expressions on their faces. Mohammed had seen enough. This night was getting stranger by the minute. He called for the elevator and waited for it farther away from the window and the handfull of people observing the fire. They saw that the elevator had been called so they followed Mohammed. They became upset when they noticed he illuminated a floor going in the opposite direction that they wanted to go. He chuckled to himself as the doors closed and reflected him in a different tone. He didn't recognize the man staring back at him. For even though his reflection was cast back at him in a gold color he noticed the color sucked from his face.

"You need some sleep." Sophia's voice snuck into his head. Or was she in the elevator with him.

The doors opened and a mass of men gathered outside the elevator. They waited until Mohammed got off then they packed themselves in and closed the door. His room was at the end of the hall. Although he wouldn't care to observe it for much longer, it provided him with a better view of the fire. He paused at the door and frantically searched for his key. Each pocket in his pants was empty or at least not pertaining the key. It wasn't until he felt his coat pocket that the key made itself known to him. He opened the door to the dark room and switched on the light. The bed was like an oasis to him. But before he could take refuge between the sheets, he had one final thing to do.

16

Japan, 1962

The sun was refreshing on this side of the world. It was not clouded by smog or haze. Its beauty originated with the lands that were so meticulously cared for. The water created a peace, as it slivered through rolling green hills, littered with pink petals falling from peach blossomed trees. The architecture was something that was renound across the world for its clear identity. Gardens of stone and metal soulfully combined to create a ease and a peace. You could see it on the faces of everyone that passed by. There wasn't an agenda or a duty that first had to be fulfilled, instead it was a serene land and ancient knowledge that guided these people. For an architect such as Mohammed this was a pilgrimage that had to be taken. Much like the pillars in his faith, this became a Hajj. For him and his family.

Japan was a distant land, one that not many Pakistani's had personally sought to find. The people rose and fell like the sun, but continually shined as bright to visitors of Mohammed's stature. Perhaps that is why they called it the land of the rising sun. He was refreshed with such a change of pace, and although it was the closest piece of heaven he had ever seen, there was only one place he could truly call home. Still his wife and daughters seemed to enjoy the people and the lifestyle that was shown to them. The results of the product that produced the people was nothing Mohammed could dismiss. He envied the system of education and government assistance that had setup such a success.

"Abu, Abu look at this picture, the hotel clerk taught me how to write my name." Shehla, Mohammed's oldest daughter, presented him with a calligraphic scribble.

"Oh, so that is how you spell your name? So this whole time you were doing it wrong."

"Look Neeloo and Zarina took Duree's and crumpled it up." Shehla continued.

"Neeloo, Zarina, Duree, come here this instance!" Mohammed yelled.

They lined up in front of him like a soldier does for his sergeant. They positioned themselves in a line that started from oldest to youngest. Since Shehla was the big mouth she was not in line. First stood Neelo, than Zarina, then Duree.

"I'm sorry Duree, you can come here." He signaled to his lap.

Duree turned around and made a face at the two other girls and jumped into her fathers arms.

"What happened to your picture?" He kindly asked his youngest.

"I don't know, Neeloo and Zarina took it without asking."

"Did you do something to make them want to take it away from you?"

Duree shook her head. Neeloo and Zarina looked at each other in amazement.

"Wait Abu that's not true!" Cried Zarina.

"Well then what happened?"

Zarina came forth as the brave one and cleared her throat as she began to unveil her story to the judge. "Well Abu she finished her picture before we could finish ours. Then she started yelling out loud that she was better than us because she finished before us. Neeloo said she wasn't and pushed her. Then Duree got up and started yelling again that she knew more than us. Which is not true Abu."

"How do you know that?"

"We go to school, and Duree stays at home, she doesn't have the knowledge that we have."

"So you go to school and you are older than her... hmm that doesn't mean she does not know more than you."

"Yes it does, doesn't it? You always say that the best people go to school and know the most about everything." Shouted Neeloo.

Shehla just rolled her eyes in the corner while listening to the nonsense. She had to be mature, it was the only way her sisters would have that concept in their lives. They all took after their mother, and like their mother they were increasingly spoiled by their father. Shehla tried very hard to make life at home easy for her father. She could see the distance of the world on her father's face. She didn't interfere with these hissy fits; instead let she let her father attend to them. While she was more than capable of quelling them she knew it provided her father with normalcy.

"I still know more than you!" Duree snickered while in the comforting embrace of her father.

"Well then smart one, tell me what you know that they do not."

"I can't."

"Why not? How will I believe that you know more than they do if you don't tell me."

"Because I am very smart."

"I know you are but they don't think that. You have to tell them something they don't know."

"Well there is one big thing that I know that nobody else knows."

"Then let us know jaan." Mohammed encouraged her.

"Yeah what is it?" Zarina stood so matter-of-factly.

"I promised her I wouldn't say anything."

"Who is she?"

Duree hesitated before continuing. She saw the smug look on both her sisters faces. Turning her gaze, she saw Shehla in the corner admiring her own work. Then she looked at her father who nodded for her to continue.

"Amma. Amma told me and didn't tell anyone else."

"Does amma want you to be smarter than everyone?"

"Well yeah, don't you?"

"Yes I do but I do not want you to rub it in."

"But it's a big secret that only I and amma know."

"Well why don't you let all of us be the judge on that. Maybe Shehla knows. Maybe Zarina, Neeloo, and I know also."

"You don't. I know that much."

"Well then if it is so important for you to use it to bicker with, than I think you should tell all of us."

"Okay. The baby in amma's stomach is a baby boy."

Mohammed was shocked to hear such news come from his daughters mouth. He never imagined it was really something that he wouldn't know. He propped Duree onto the floor and got out of his chair. In his search for his wife he didn't even think to hand out a judgment or punishment for his daughters like he usually would. This was news that had to be acknowledged. He knew, that his wife didn't know that he knew. It was a kind and cruel trick. He was trying to figure out a way of breaking the news, while breaking it back to Sophia. A boy. At long last from among his children a boy would follow in his footsteps. He was so anxious to know everything now. Sophia was clever in telling Duree. She knew how to keep a secret better than the other girls. Mohammed knew that she purposefully told the youngest so that this scene would create a jolly mood for him. She was smarter than he knew. Of all the years she had been by his side, the cruelest trick she played was really the sweetest one.

Sophia was sitting near the dual vanity sink fixing her hair. Mohammed stormed in and sat silently and with a hidden smirk. She didn't know how Mohammed could possibly be angry, after all they were in Japan on a beautiful day culminated with beautiful news. He didn't say anything or even hint at a smile. He just walked up behind her and hugged her. She watched and waited as she felt his arms feeling for the baby to kick.

"Do you know what you want to name him?"

He didn't say a word for he had a secret that he didn't want her to know…yet.

"I…don't know."

Sophia knew better.

"Tell me. I know you know."

"I have no idea what to think."

"Yes you do. It is something you have thought about for many days."

"Rehan. I like Rehan. Of course he will carry my name, but it will be Mohammed Rehan Ahmed."

"See I told you." It became difficult to keep things from Sophia as the days they spent together grew. She didn't have the education that he wanted his daughters to get. She however was taught in forms of different things that could not be simply re-educated. Although she was a housewife, she was much more than a push over. "I always know especially if it is coming from you."

"You can read me like a book?"

"Like the Quran!" she replied with a hard tone.

Mohammed held onto her stomach and looked at her through the mirror. It was miraculous how Sophia's intuition as a mother had always been correct and always stopped the guessing game.

"Don't worry Mohammed, we will be back in Pakistan by the time he is ready to be born."

"How did you know I was thin—"

"Like the Quran! I told you. You are too easy."

Mohammed let go of Sophia and stretched his arms from windowpane to windowpane near the view overlooking Japan. He breathed in a newfound glory, as he was the lord of a new land. He cherished each one of his children and their individuality. This was his moment to properly invite a new one into his mind. He couldn't lie to himself. Mohammed often thought of raising a son who would protect his family in his absence. It was a duty fit for a son, not a servant, or a gatekeeper, or a driver. He had tried his hardest to treat his daughters as girls. Even though they had come out as perfect as he imagined, there was no denying the void they created when aspects true to the nature of boys arose. He could not take his daughters to hunt with him or even to a cricket match. No longer did he have to convey a strict devotion his daughter's ambiguity. His ambitions were going to be channeled through a boy. His son. Mohammed Rehan Ahmed.

Their vacation was just ending but his greatest feelings were yet to be expressed. He wanted to shout from the rooftop all the way back to Karachi. His voice would be heard one way or another.

The phone rang in the other room, Mohammed could not be found to pick it up. Instead Shehla took over as the next oldest and answered.

His daughter summoned Mohammed to the phone. He was surprised his voice had reached Karachi so fast. It didn't matter who it was, the servant, Jamal, even Faraz. This news was to be shared.

"This is Mohammed."

"Mohammed." The proverbial voice slewed on the line.

"Oh, Nasir." He recognized his cousin's voice.

"There is something you need to know before you come back to Karachi."

"Well we arrive in a few days. Can this wait?"

"I think you need to know."

"Well Nasir there is something that I would like you to know."

Nasir sensed Mohammed's attitude and intervened before he could. "Your school on Tariq road. It has crumbled to the ground."

The line stayed quiet for a minute, and there was nothing Mohammed wanted to say. Not even the eminent news he had just learned.

17

Pakistan, 1962

Crumbled wasn't the word that should have been used over the phone. Torn, Ripped, Blown, Shattered, these were more proper words to use. The school was only meant for grade school. It was to be the launching point of their new lives. While it was a modest school that took in modest children, it was not a mill. It was two stories high. Mohammed personally installed and inspected the structure and support beams inside, there was no way he could have overseen something so unsound. Blocks of cement were either being cleaned off the street or pawned for a lower price, Mohammed couldn't tell. Children that were supposed to be taking lessons in the school attacked Mohammed and his peers for money. As Mohammed passed through them he didn't even care that he was being pick pocketed hidden with hugs and cries. Fathers and mothers scavenged the scene looking for survivors or any sign of them. Mohammed could tell right away who had lost someone and who was still waiting.

It looked as if the building were cut perfectly down the middle with a swift blow from an axe. The shops were at least still cleaned, but the children in the street and the beggar-parents remained. Policemen who were sent to scatter the scene were positioned next to tea and sweet shops. The only people smiling were actors and models on the billboards above.

"Perhaps the land below wasn't as sturdy as we were led to believe." One of his coworkers commented from within the crowd gathering behind Mohammed.

"This wasn't done naturally. The support post, the land, the materials, they were all checked."

Jamal split the crowd like the red sea and walked to Mohammed's back. He reached for his shoulder to comfort him. As he touched it Mohammed moved toward the building and a large stone that lay on the ground in the middle of the street. He picked up the jagged piece and broke off a smaller piece of the cement or at least what he was led to believe was cement. It was the one thing he didn't look over. It crumbled into smaller pieces with the pressing of his fingers. It wouldn't hold the pressure Mohammed applied with his hands. The words of his professor back at Cornell whisked into his mind. 'The world is structurally unsound.'

"Jamal. What is this?" Mohammed questioned without looking back.

"That is cement." Jamal thought the question was rhetorical.

"I know that but what is this mixed in between? Is this type 3 or type 1?"

"I used type 2."

Mohammed didn't want to believe what he just heard. It was bad enough his hand was forced to pick Jamal for such a task. Jamal was the last person he wanted to put in charge of this project. There was no one else that knew cement like he did except for Mohammed. Unfortunately for Mohammed there was no one who would accept bribes like he did. Jamal had failed him, for the last time.

"Type 2 is not to be used in a moist climate. What's more it seems to have been mixed with a weaker mortar bind."

Jamal was shocked that Mohammed knew more about cement then he did. "That is not entirely true. Type 2 can be used in any environment."

"Not when it is bound like this!" He got up from his crouching position and threw the stone at Jamal's feet. The crowd behind him drew back. It was the perfect time for Mohammed to finally lash out. "I am at wits end Jamal. I give you a small task to complete, and you even think to cut corners there. Once, just once did I want you to be completely honest and humble! Instead you launder money through a government-assisted fund to put more in your wallet. You should pray that God has such ascribed mercy; for now you shall receive none from me...you are a coward Jamal, a small, indecent speck of dust that holds no regard for life. These are children Jamal. Our children, the children of Pakistan and of Karachi, and instead of helping build them up, you strip away the core and pit of their hearts and minds. Your need for wealth is like the sea needing more water in its basin. You have plagued this city for the last time Jamal. God forgive your mother for bearing through your birth, and God damn your father to hell for teaching you nothing about decency."

He walked back toward the small piles of stones littered all over the street. It shifted traffic, but that was the only thing it seemed to stop.

Jamal's silence made his guilt ooze from his skin like sweat on a hot day.

"You are responsible for cleaning this up, in my report I will state that." Mohammed stated. "Once the cement is picked off of the ground, under your supervision will the lot be cleared and materials be sold. After the materials have been sold you will take your car to the dealer and sell it, along with anything else it will take to recuperate the money lost. Once you have done all that I want you to collapse this lot underneath itself. Am I understood?"

Jamal said nothing and didn't move or give a sign of agreement.

"Or should I take your life right now?" Mohammed reproached Jamal who countered with a wince.

"You think I am not afraid to take your life. Why not? The police can be bought off like anything else in this city. I have friends in very high places, I'm sure you will not be missed. All I have to do is tell the crowd gathered not ten feet behind you that this was solely your fault…I told you never to bring anything like this to my knowledge again. Now I must treat you like a donkey. Do you know what happens to a donkey when it becomes lame?" He didn't say anything. "Jamal if you want me to spare your life, answer me when I am talking to you."

"It's…gutted." Jamal sputtered.

"It's gutted that's right…when you are done doing all that I have mandated, I will have your job, and Nasir's and Saleem's, and anyone else's who was involved."

He walked back to the crowd and picked out Nasir and Saleem from within. "Help him look for survivors. Your lives depend on it." He demanded as he walked back to his car.

Jamal, Nasir and Saleem gathered near the rubble and looked at what their greed had bought them.

"Why don't we just tell them it was Mohammed's fault?" Saleem asked

"They respect him too much to believe that." Jamal pointed to the people around him.

They had nearly escaped the scene and made it back to their warm and secure homes. They had to lay to their souls to waste while mixing and searching for the crushed children. They were handed torches like discovers entering in to a forbidden land. The only chance of a triumphant return would have to be with every child unscathed. They were greeted with the faces and families of the children marred by the collapsed building. The screams of people still being ripped from the ground like a weed being pulled from the soil became a reality. They had no place their money or its sponsors could hide them. At least for one night in the midst of anguish Pakistan would have its retribution.

18

Pakistan, 1963

Dawn was approaching, that much was clear. Mohammed's entire home was the first thing in this part of Karachi to welcome in and see off the sun. He was in his son's room trying to rock him back to sleep. This was usually Sophia's affair, however ever since Rehan was born he couldn't help but spend as much time with his son as possible. It was an understatement to say that he loved his children; this was the prime age that they would get to know their father. He loved holding his son and humming him traditional types of nursery rhymes. The vibrations of his voice provided him a calm and simplicity, much to the liking of all his children. He would sit in the rocking chair next to window and wait at least a few extra minutes until he was sure that the baby was asleep. Rehan was a fussier baby falling asleep than Mohammed was used to from the experiences with his daughters. After singing him to sleep

Mohammed would have to put his left heel up onto his right knee and create a pocket that Rehan would nestle himself into. It was the one moment of peace Mohammed could have each and every day before he left for work.

"You've gotten him too used to that." Sophia whispered trying not to wake him. She didn't want Mohammed to know, but she would always creep in and catch a glimpse of Mohammed and Rehan. She couldn't help but interrupt this time. They looked like they belonged in silence and in each other's embrace.

"He will soon grow out of it and find a more comfortable outlet. Just like all the other children." Mohammed hinted with a shred of misery.

"And like all the other children they will love you for the type of father you have been." Sophia said trying to bring up his spirits.

Rehan opened his eyes and adjusted it to the sight of his parents looking over him. Sophia was too far away for him to make a complete figure out of. Mohammed was in a much better area of interest. He just looked and examined everything that his face had to offer.

Mohammed watched as he would try and fail to reach his face. He was young but the intuition of the world was slowly unveiling itself. Although it was time for him to fall back asleep there was no denying the feeling he created for Mohammed when he was awake. There was an ounce of recognition between the two. Mohammed did love all his children equally but this the best time to bond with his children. Rehan would do as the rest of his siblings did and lay silently as Mohammed would regale him with tales of his family and ancestors. Mohammed however was stuck like stone in the gaze of his son. He couldn't explain the hold it had on him even if he wanted it to. Neither of them smiled and tried to make more of the situation than was already at hand. There were no words, no gestures, just a father looking down to his son while trying to familiarize himself with *his* father. Sophia was saying something but Mohammed didn't notice. He would just nod and pretend to respond. He would have to cherish this moment, for when Rehan was to grow Mohammed's love would have to become that of a stern voice, and stern resolve.

His family was together in the same home, even though most of them were asleep. Time held no purpose. It was just a father his son and the rising sun left to greet and accept the world.

19

"Who's is this?" Mohammed demanded as he stood over a suitcase outside home. "Sophia call the servants. I want to know who this belongs to." He yelled across the house. No one responded, and he didn't dare go outside the confines of his house to find out what it contained. It just propped itself up menacingly directly in the middle of Mohammed's courtyard. It was strange to say the least, and deadly to say the most. It was hardest thing Mohammed had ever had to look at, because it was so close to his house and so far from his grasp.

"What is it sahib?" Mohammed's servant entered to break the scene.

"What is that, who does that belong to?" Mohammed whispered.

"Perhaps it is one of your wife's."

"Don't be a fool. None of hers are that color." He spoke to the golden shine bleeding into his home.

"I shall go ask every servant."

"Ask the gatekeeper first." Mohammed stopped him before going on an unnecessarily long quest. "Use the back door." He pushed him along his way.

The servant left his side as exited through the butler pantry onto the hill next to the home.

Mohammed stood his ground. He was like a knight examining his enemy before attacking, except his shield was his teacup and his sword was his newspaper. The game of standstill continued between Mohammed and the suitcase. He tried to drown out the sound around him and focus on any sound he could hear coming from the within the golden case. There was no ticking or sound of gas leaking. It was just the unavoidable sound of silence. Rehan ran up to his side and saw the door was open. He tried like any eight-year-old child to go outside. He opened the swinging screen door and put one foot on the courtyard floor.

"Rehan no!" Mohammed grabbed his son and pulled him back inside. He didn't realize the pressure it had on his arm until Rehan started to whimper. He didn't bother apologizing or letting loose his grip. He commanded, "Go find Shehla and play with her."

Rehan ran as quickly as he could up the stairwell and out of sight. Mohammed's home was very large, and the inside was the only place he knew of where his family would truly be safe.

The gatekeeper swept his steps behind him all the way up to Mohammed. Usually he had to take off his shoes, but this was urgent as was described to him by the servant.

Before he reached Mohammed's side he was already being questioned. "What is that? I want to know whom that belongs to. Was it delivered? What is in it?"

"It…um…the." The gatekeeper couldn't find the words quickly enough to satisfy Mohammed.

"Speak swiftly."

"It was delivered by a car, sahib."

"Who's car was it, what color was it, who was in the car?"

"I don't know, sahib, it was just a black car and only a driver came to the gate. I took it from him and placed it there like he said."

"What else did he say?"

"Nothing else sahib, just that it was only supposed to be opened by you." The servant replied frantically as if he were on the verge of being struck.

"I want you to stay here and guard the door. Do not let any of my children or Sophia out! Understand!" Mohammed's hands were already sweating heavier than his brow. Each step he took toward the suitcase was an undesired eternity. His heart took at least ten beats in between each step. He would pause at each interval to listen for some sign of the suitcase making noise. He thought he had singled in on a ticking sound coming from it, but it turned out to only be his watch. He didn't take his eyes or mind off of the package before him. When the base of the suitcase was begging at his feet, he reached down with great uncertainty and picked it up. It was much lighter than he had thought, but that still did not make it less dangerous. Mohammed held it away from his body. He carried it farther out into the courtyard and farther away from peering eyes, as his children looked on from the bedroom windows on the second floor. Setting the case on its side in the grass he said a small prayer of safe keeping to himself before opening it. 'Click.' The sound was small yet devastating. Another 'click' and the suitcase was open. He pushed the two sides apart and saw what it was. It was money. Dirty, thin, sharp, strapped money. He wasn't as surprised as he thought he was going to be, because part of him was hoping it was a bomb. There was no feeling of doubt, or regret in opening it, just a serene tear in his heart. A note was folded at the top of the currency. He didn't have to guess who it was from, he knew Faraz was behind this daring act. He could smell his scent from the second the air was let out of the case. At least Mohammed had won a bet with himself. He knew that Faraz would resort to desperate measures. He locked it up without laying a finger on the vast rows of bills smiling back at him. Locked in the darkness they would remain, never to see Mohammed's hand again. Mohammed returned to the house with the suitcase in his hands. He called for the gatekeeper who was still cleaning the mud on the floor with the help of the servant.

"Yes sahib."

"Was the car similar to my silver car?" Mohammed began to take clever guesses.

"It was. Only black."

"Did the driver have a mustache like yours only thinner?"

"He did. Only thinner like you say."

"Did he have a birth mark on his right ear? Clearly noticeable."

"Yes sahib. How did you know?"

Mohammed had many run-ins with Faraz to know much about him. Like any businessman Mohammed would access all aspects of the situation during his engagements.

He wasn't enraged at all, for he knew that Faraz would eventually succumb to this. In fact Mohammed had all but executed his plan on what he would do given this very situation. He called on his gatekeeper with a very large smile.

"Yes sahib." He was already near by.

"Did the driver see you place this by the courtyard?"

"No sahib."

Mohammed was getting giddy and excited as each question he asked was received with an equally satisfying answer. "I have a very important task for you. First I need you to go and get my driver."

The gatekeeper was already on his way before Mohammed finished speaking his request.

He looked again at the case and made sure no one was around him. He reopened it and pulled out the note he didn't care to read and crumpled it in his hands and threw it into the pond within his courtyard. When he relocked it his driver and gatekeeper came to his side.

"I need you to do something for me. Something very, very important."

The two just stood candidly nodding their heads in agreement.

"I need you to take me to Tariq road. I need both of you to come with me, you know where the crumbled school is?"

The driver nodded again.

"I want you to accompany me to Tariq road. Both of you go get the car and meet me in the drive."

They nodded their heads with more enthusiasm. They nearly leapt into the drive to begin their heeded quest. Mohammed sat the case on the steps near the door and found his servant inside the home cleaning dishes. Mohammed approached him calmly but was much more straightforward in talking to him.

"I am going for a drive, let Sophia know I will be back in a few hours."

"What was in the suitcase sahib?"

"Just some plans for the future is all. Start dinner and don't let them eat without me."

The car honked its horn when it came to the front. Mohammed didn't say goodbye to his family although he knew most his children had already seen him on his way. The gatekeeper was inside the car already. Mohammed got in and closed the door. Without word of beginning the trip the car was already in motion. Mohammed sat in the back like a child who was about to attend his own birthday party. As the car ran through familiar areas in familiar settings Mohammed reveled in his idea.

He looked around at mosques accompanied with movie billboards and schools purchased by wealthy landowners he began to think to himself 'Times had radically changed. The amount of time it took for that change to occur is equally foreboding. Traditional values are as worthless as the people that hold them in their minds. There are no longer any deeds worthy of carrying a blood right, the impatience of solidarity is justified by the greed behind the ever weakening rupee. With it bribes came in larger quantities rather than a larger worth.'

The car stopped. It was the quickest long ride he had ever taken. His mind was juggling the thoughts of a new Pakistan along with the change he was about to create. The car was parked in its usual corner. Mohammed looked at the partially cleaned corner, formally the school he had built. Scrambling atop the rounded pyramid of cement were the three wise men, (as he had come to refer to them) Jamal, Nasir and Saleem. He had even brought them a gift.

Mohammed looked out of the window to see where all the children had hidden away. He found it odd that his car wasn't being attacked. He tried to see through the endless hallways in the covered bazaars. The only hint of children he could find were the flashes of their scurry bodies dissected by them running in between the pillars of each storefront. The street had the symptoms of improvement. The streets were now fully paved and open to several new lanes. Mohammed began to think that the children and poor were tired of coming to his car altogether, now they had to be quick, solitary, and even more pitiful than the next one. Sharing money was beginning to put itself out of the picture. That was about to change.

Mohammed asked to be joined in the back by his driver and gatekeeper, they did so without opening the door. They waited for the other to slip into the backseat next to Mohammed before the other made his move. Once they were all cozy and ready to focus Mohammed relayed the next step in his plan. With the eyes of the gatekeeper on the suitcase and the mind of the driver on the road he told them what had to be done. They just listened and figured out how to please their master's request. "Now go." Mohammed commanded.

The driver opened the door and stepped out of the car, he was followed by the gatekeeper. Mohammed stayed in the car until the opportune moment. The driver disappeared into the bazaar as the gatekeeper headed toward the pile of rubble next to the three wise men. It only took a few seconds for Mohammed to know that his plan had began to catch attention. He could hear screams and the sound of people gathering. Suddenly the driver ran out to the middle of the crowded street with a procession of followers. When he reached the point where he could go no farther he opened up his jacket he had been protecting and let out an avalanche of money. The people jumped on the pile like a pack of starving rats on rotting meat. The driver began to laugh as he saw all the children and women smile as they filled their pockets, bags, hands, hats- anything they could use- with money.

Mohammed stepped out of the car and saw that the crowd had gathered the attention of the three men cleaning up on the hill. He saw his gatekeeper reach the part of the mound where they were standing and waiting. He then watched as the gatekeeper handed them each a single rupee, and profess to each the exact words Mohammed had told him to: "Mohammed believed it would be fair that you receive some of that money." He pointed to the furious mob still scavenging for money.

Mohammad saw he had gained notoriety from Jamal, Saleem, and Nasir, so he pulled out a thick stack of more money from his pockets and held it up for them to see. He nodded and waited for the same response from his gatekeeper at the top of the hill. With all his might Mohammed floated the pile into the air. It quickly dispersed as it hit its apex and began to fall back to the Earth. People from everywhere had gathered there was not a single empty spot on the street. All the shops had emptied out the only people left without a taste were the three men at the top of the hill.

Mohammed knew it was cruel, but so was the life those men had sentenced these same people to.

Saleem and Nasir put the money in their pockets and started to work again. Jamal put down his shovel and walked down to the low point of the hill. He still had his rupee with him, it was still in his hand, it was still in his mind. He watched as the sea of people moved wave after wave back and forth looking for the next free bill. Through it all was Mohammed clearly still and visible in his white shalwaar. Jamal knew as long as Mohammed was there that he couldn't try and make for any of the money. He also knew that Mohammed would not budge until each piece of currency had found a new home. He turned back to go to the top of the hill squeezing the rupee with great force. Reaching the top, the imprint of the coin left on his hand was that of the president of Pakistan. Although he could still feel Mohammed's gaze upon him he clenched it even harder then with all his might, threw it into the crowd. It fell upon them without concern and with ease. He grabbed his lonely shovel and joined the other two working on the top. He started digging harder and faster, without a known outcome and without a goal. With each pile unearthed with his shovel and with each numbing moment in his hands the peasants below were being shut out. He just continued to dig, and dig until Mohammed could no longer see him; until the world could no longer find him.

20

December 18, 1973

The line was dead, that was something that Mohammed had to continually live with in any hotel he was visiting. The only glimpse of light that snuck its way into his room was the flashing ones coming from outside the hotel entrance. That and the fire. He liked to dim the room and keep it as dark as possible during the night. Light was an unwanted noise. Too often and too long had he been away from his family. He hung up the phone and tried again. It was dead.

"Who the hell would be using the lines this late at night?" He thought to himself.

He figured that a hotel this size had to at least keep five lines free at all time, and to conserve power would shift to three at night. But still it was ridiculous, Mohammed thought, that someone or some people would be on the phone this late. It made no difference to him what the calls were being used for, nothing was more important to him than to hear a familiar voice of any member of his family. It was no use, he figured he might as well try again in a few minutes. He loosened his tie as he began to feel hot, the small migraine and dizziness he experienced in the stairwell had reintroduced itself. "Why am I feeling this way?" Trying to find some sort of solace he rubbed his hands together for warmth and then pressed and rubbed them against his temples.

"I didn't rub them that hard." He looked and felt as his hands began to sweat. The beating of his heart picked up in sound and pace. Thumping again and again, Mohammed believed it to be the lack of sleep getting to him. He uncuffed his shirt and rolled his sleeves up to his elbows. His head began to pound so he went into the bathroom to wet a hand towel with warm water. He squeezed the excess water into the sink and carried it out to the bed. He laid down and placed the warm towel on his eyes and forehead. It provided him with little comfort, for it only caused his heart to calm. His head still pounded, and he could feel each bead of sweat form in the midst of his palms. He closed his eyes but his thoughts brought light to the pounding in his head and body. With each pound came a burst of light in his mind. Trying to turn to each side, he was searching for any means of comfort. It was of no use, he had to try and contact his family, perhaps that was the best medicine.

The phone rang once, he was surprised. Had his calls of pain reached all the way to Karachi? He anticipated it to ring one more time before he tried to pick it up. It didn't. He reached over the nightstand and picked up the phone. There was no voice but the phone did come alive.

With a new impulse Mohammed rose to sit at the edge of the bed while trying desperately to get hold of an operator. The phone was continually withdrawn and then placed on the receiver. He hoped this was the way to attract some attention. Finally Mohammed waited a few seconds after picking up the phone. He then heard a woman's voice on the other side.

"Destination of your call?" The operator asked.

Mohammed thought he was still imagining the voice.

"Destination of your call? Please?" The operator became forceful.

"Oh, Karachi please."

"Hold please."

The line went silent for a moment and then arose again.

"Destination in Karachi please."

"Founders Road. Ahmed Housing. Block A." Finally he was going to get through.,,

A crow in a tree within the courtyard stared down at Neeloofur. She stood there with no sense of hostility or pride, waiting to chase the bird as it prepared to fly. It did no such thing. She watched as its talons grabbed hold of the branch so tight it ripped the bark from the tree.

"Fly away crow, don't come near!" Neeloofur loudly commanded.

The crow tilted its head and focused directly on Neeloofur. It opened its mouth and let out a shrieking scream that seemed as if it could shatter the windows in the house.

It did not faze Neeloofur, tho, she stood her ground. "Fly away crow, don't scream again!" Neeloofur commanded again as she reached down to pick up a rock.

The crow witnessed her new weapon and taunted Neeloofur by hoping along closer to her while staying on the branch. Its eyes became human, and blood shot. It looked up to the clouds and shrieked again. There was no shattering this time just a wave of darkness from above. After a blink of light the single crow was surrounded by thousands of other crows. Crows now took any empty casing of branches on the tree in the courtyard. The loud sound of a united force rambling to each other overwhelmed the barren courtyard. Each crow focused its undying attention upon the helpless girl.

Neeloofur now stood against the black tree with a single rock in her hand. She clenched it and held her breath. Then she unleashed it upon any bird that would find its way in the path of the hurled rock. As she let go she closed her eyes. She listened as she heard it hit one bird, then an even louder sound as that one bird smashed to the ground. When she opened her eyes, the birds still on the branch looking down at the fallen one confronted her. She ran to its aid, no longer afraid. She only meant to shoo it away instead it lay lifeless and peaceful on the ground. She picked it up and held it close. The other birds on the tree continued looking on. Then the original shrieking crow flew down next to her. As she was crouched the crow bowed its head to the other dead crow and cried a tear of blood that evaporated into the soil. Neeloofur began to cry. And cry. And cry. "Help me crow, help me!"

The crow didn't move, it just flapped its wings and hovered in a circle above Neeloofur's head. It beckoned to the other crows and was joined in flight. They all flew away. The other crows followed their leader and left Neeloofur alone with her deed in her hands. Still she wept.

"Wake up crow, wake up and fly away!"

It lay unmoving in her hands and grinned as if it knew what she did not.

"Please crow, fly away. Fly away!"

"Neeloo wake up!" Shehla began shaking her violently. "Its just a dream!"

Neeloofur woke up and peered around the darkened room. Shehla was above her holding her shoulders and shaking her awake.

"What…I was…" Neeloofur looked around and was immediately struck by the familiarity of her room. The light by her bed was turned on and everything else remained unnoticed.

"It was just a dream Neeloofur. You were crying and screaming so loud. It was just a dream." Shehla reassured her.

"Was I… Was this…"

"Yes it was a dream, its okay." Shehla comforted her as she hugged her, she couldn't help but inquire: "What were you dreaming about anyway?"

"I can't explain it, I can't even remember what happened." Neeloofur exclaimed as she tried to grab hold of her situation. She was in her room and the night was late. The sun hadn't even given a hint of where it was to peak. Neeloofur began to calm slowly. The clock in her room showed a time that Neeloofur had only ever seen a couple of times in person.

"Are you okay?" Shehla asked.

"I think I am okay." Neeloofur gently pushed Shehla's hands away.

Shehla remained confused but knew that bad dreams held a place in the mind for much longer than some things. She went back to the bed on her side of the room and sat waiting for Neeloofur to reassure her before trying for sleep again. "Do you want me to get you some water?"

Neeloofur didn't respond.

"It was so real, I felt like it was something that I had done before."

"Dreams are strange. Abu said it's a way for us to know there is something greater beyond us."

"Even the bad ones?" Neeloofur asked.

"I suppose. With every good thing has to come a bad thing…Are you sure you are alright?"

"Yes I think I am okay. Thank you. Go back to sleep." Just as Neeloofur said that the phone rang twice then held still. Since it was late one of the girls had to go for it. Shehla waited for it to ring again. So did the rest of the house. Nothing was heard.

All remained quiet with an uneasy serenity in the Karachi home for the rest of the evening.

"Damn it, not again!" Mohammed shouted into the phone.

"Sorry sir." The operator came back on the phone. "It seems like the connection is weak from your area. I believe they are working on fixing that, and it should be fully respectable in a few days. However I can try it again for you."

"That's alright, I was going to try again in the morning." Mohammed knew that was just an excuse for the phone operators just not to try harder. He hung up the phone and laid back down with the towel pressed against his head.

"God grant me patience." Mohammed proclaimed to the heavens. He closed his eyes and tried to find some outlet of thought to relieve the pain. Focus would dissect the pain. "Why am I feeling this way?" He thought of work, and his life. His thoughts drifted in and out but mostly around his children, he began to think of each one. Shehla, she was his oldest and bravest; his little leader. Neeloofur, the next in line, she was so smart and intuitive. Zarina, the boldest and most assertive. Duree, his youngest daughter, the most creative and daring. Then of course he looked upon the face of his son Rehan, his son, what more could be said about the boy who was every bit of decency a father could imagine for his son. The pain in his head faded when he came to the next person in line- Sophia. How she was everything he was not, and how she was every bit the person he imagined he would grow old with. His pain died away for a moment, only a moment. The peace which he sought out was now gone and his head began to pound harder and harder. There was no possible way he was going to rest or even fall asleep with the type of pain he was experiencing. He squirmed to the base of his bed and searched for his suitcase. It was partially hidden under the side of the bed and it was peeked open. Ripping it open he searched for pills, a salve, anything he knew his wife would've snuck into the bag. Nothing. His only hope was to either call for the front office or sit and wait until the pain passed. Neither seemed logical and only one was a reality. He positioned himself back on the bed and put the now-cold towel on his head. Even trying to think of his family was not working to sooth the pain. His heart was pounding faster, his palms were drenched, and each portion of his body ached.

"God grant me patience. Someone please give me patience." Mohammed prayed. And prayed. Waiting for a miracle to knock at his door. Waiting for some sort of divine intervention.

21

Mohammed was at the top of the building he had created. Finally, he believed, he earned the right to look over all the planning and architecture that Karachi was to take part in. He had all but wiped out the bribes flowing in and out of this branch of government. However there was only so much one mans influence could have over the masses. His office was perched at the end of a hallway at the top of the fifteenth floor overlooking the sea and the city. He had managed to rid the office of the Jamal's, and the Nasir's and the Saleem's. As far as he knew they had found some work in the newly formed Bangladesh. He didn't dwell on them for too long for it would only bring anger into his heart. At long last he was able to give this office what it was truly lacking. He was busy sifting through the rest of their remaining work looking for projects worthy of Mohammed's new position.

The phone rang. And rang again.

He picked it up. "Mohammed Ahmed."

"Salaam Jaan its me." Sophia's words bursted through the line.

"Salaam Jaan." He was always relieved to hear her voice.

"There is something that requires your attention."

"Can it wait until I get home?"

"As you requested you wanted to be the first to know when something like this happened."

Mohammed set down the papers in his hands and focused peculiarly on the phone. "Alright go ahead."

"One of the children came home with low marks."

"Low marks! Who?"

"Well I was as surprised as you were but it was—"

"Rehan? Was it Rehan?"

"No. Actually it was Duree."

"Duree? That's impossible." Mohammed knew she was smart; she was always at the top of her class. In fact he pampered her because of her gift in school and studies. It came as huge shock to Mohammed.

"Yes."

"How low is low?"

"It seems that she is at an impasse of perhaps retaking a course."

"Put her on the phone!"

He heard a shuffle in the background of the line. He could hear a whimper followed by a yell and a command. A hand took hold of the phone: "Abu." The voice barely came through. He prepared his seldom used stern voice.

"Duree! What happened?"

"I cannot say for sure, Abu. I finished the work you even helped me out on my assignments, I stayed late and even got help on the work I could not figure out. The only thing I can think of is the two assignments missed when we were in Lahore."

Mohammed thought back to when he took his family for a retreat to Lahore. He valued their studies and knowledge above all else, sometimes even religion. He didn't like to think that he was the reason for any type of failure. He wanted to be angry but he would only wind up taking it out on himself, or maybe this was just her way of getting out of trouble. He began to line up questions he would ask when he got home. 'When was this assignment handed out and when was it due?' 'Are you sure you worked as hard as you could?' He would even grade it himself. His control would only find an end once she would confess.

The line stayed quiet until a cough brought Mohammed back to the phone. It was no use arguing over the phone, even though he knew what he would eventually discover, "We will take a look at all your work when I get home."

"Okay Abu." She sounded relieved at the tone of his voice.

He hung up the phone and returned to his work without hesitation. He was now involved in the planning of Islamabad. The city had just begun to expand rapidly. It had drawn all sorts of attention from all sorts of interest groups. Mohammed was interested in developing the new capital of Pakistan. It, however, was an extremely dangerous proposition. The ground was stable in parts, and in others (where new interests arose) fault lines crossed. Mohammed as well as many others knew this area was not to be taken lightly. Any movement from the earth and years of work would tumble to the ground. It seemed that his opinion would be the one guiding thought to push or pull anyone off the fence. In his heart he knew what his final decision was going to be. He was focused on Karachi, and would have to phone in his denial to Islamabad.

His office was higher than his previous one and the sound of traffic echoed and buzzed at a greater volume. It was the only drawback to this office. He personally recreated this office. His was the only room that had any type of privacy. All the other offices had clear partitions and neatly aligned doors so that he could see everything that was going on. Mohammed did not allow any blinds or covers of any sort; he was in complete control of this office. It was also the way in which he could receive each guest coming into the office, and what a guest Mohammed had to unknowingly receive today. He could sense his presence from the minute he stepped foot on the office floor. The gold chain around his neck clanked together with each step. His greasy mustache and ever fattening face jiggled along the bordered partitions. Then there was the three-piece suit, always the three-piece suit. Faraz didn't even bother waiting to be received.

Mohammed didn't bother looking up to greet him. "Always a surprise. You yourself are not, but the manner in which we have become accustom seems to be a surprise."

"Shock keeps us active and alert."

"It can also kill a man."

"Precisely." Faraz responded the room went silent through the two. Only phones being answered and men arguing down the hall could be heard. Faraz looked at Mohammed's desk and saw the clutter, he knew how busy Mohammed had become after refusing his offers. "I called."

"Calling and speaking to someone are two completely different things."

"So it seems." Faraz laughed.

"I haven't seen you on Tariq road for a while."

"Fortunately, Tariq road is not the only street in this city."

"Yes but it is the most amazing one, wouldn't you say? From sea to city and from city to farm."

"The school is built, the road is fixed. There are many other things that have to be attended to."

"I haven't seen you at Jummah either."

"Jummah?" Mohammed knew Faraz was always inquiring about Mohammed's whereabouts. "Well you would be hard pressed to find the same person in the same mosque on the same day each week, given the number of mosques in the city."

"That, or you just have not been going."

Mohammed had come closely to knowing Faraz's wit. It, however, was not as amusing as Faraz was led to believe. "How are your mills operating?"

"Well, you know how hard it is to conduct business outside the city lines. I have to surround myself with people I can trust. So in that respect profits are thin. Although when we have what God has blessed us with, it is hard to complain, is it not?"

"Indeed it is."

"I was thinking of building in Islamabad after I was asked to bring you this." Faraz reached over the table and handed Mohammed a fancily decorated letter. "I hope you don't mind. I opened it for you."

Mohammed opened the folded letter. He read the black razed lettering out loud: "The International Architectural and Developmental Organization. You were asked to bring this to me, or you felt you had to bring it to me?"

"What is the difference? You and I are now brothers with the same respects."

"Its an invitation."

"To what?"

"A convention of the finest builders and humanitarians on this side of the world."

Mohammed was still looking at the letter. "Islamabad?"

"Well actually that is why I am here. You have to first receive an honor here then take that recognition with you to Islamabad."

"Why are you delivering this to me? I would think you would send your driver or have it mailed. What does this have to do with you?"

"Well you're not the only one with humane intentions. I was receiving my invitation to the Karachi reception and saw that you were one of only three invited to Islamabad on top of receiving an honor at the Karachi reception." He looked directly into Mohammed's eyes, "Information like that can't be bought."

"So you decided to make this trip to my office to give me an invitation."

"Oh yes. I thought you would enjoy being ahead of the curb every once and awhile. After all that is something that always helps the Master Planner for the KDA. It also helps receiving the news with one of your friends around doesn't it?"

"Friend is a strong word Faraz, and it is especially one that only acquaintances tend to over-use."

Faraz scrunched up his face. "I know that you have been in talks regarding Islamabad's development. Think of this as just my way of congratulating you on your successes. Now you get to see first hand what the future of Pakistan will look like."

"Faraz, I know this is not the reason you are here. Where is your suitcase full of money, or your treasure hunt proposal?"

"Not this time Mohammed. I have no intention of bothering you with those things. After all you will always be the one to cast the first stone."

"Yes. Better that then a pile full of money."

"Indeed." Faraz redirected.

Both the stubborn men stood their ground and played the ever-growing match of breaking silence. Mohammed pretended to be fixed on his work; while Faraz jittered with his coat and pant pockets. Mohammed knew that there was still a tension with Faraz over the money he gave away. Faraz knew it as well. Their odd esteem for each other was quickly diminished by the small war between them. Mohammed was not about to ask Faraz to leave, and Faraz was not about to take his leave. Seconds of tension turned to minutes of frustration. That was until a familiar and unwanted voice broke in.

"Here are the documents you requested." The heavy voice attacked Mohammed, but was focused on Faraz.

"Oh you remember Jamal?" Faraz slipped in.

"Jamal?" It was a figure he had not seen in a relatively long time, one Mohammed hoped to never look upon again.

The obliterated man stood in the doorway. There he was the reverse story of success. From king to pauper. From mountain top to wasteland. "Here you are." Jamal handed Faraz some papers; never making eye contact with Mohammed.

"Don't be alarmed Mohammed, he is not here for you. He works for me now."

"Works for you? Doing what exactly?"

"Oh the type of business I am in requires all sorts of talents. You never know when one might need his... passion for work."

"So he works in one of your mills?"

"That and other things... I think of him more as a hard worker."

"You mean servant!" Mohammed was on the verge of throwing both of the men out of his office. He clinched a pencil in his hands and nearly broke it in half. Given the circumstance, he was beyond himself.

"I was just waiting for Jamal before I left. I hope I didn't bother you too much."

Faraz's ways were sometimes too much to handle. For Mohammed, Faraz's methods were as unwarranted as he was. He was not prepared to welcome a banished man into his office.

The Faraz stood up and joined Jamal, Mohammed copied them but did not see them out. He did not shake his hand, or pretend to care about his departure. He just stood and looked at Jamal while Jamal had his head down and waited for Faraz to pass in front of him.

Mohammed wanted to jump at Jamal's throat. He couldn't. He never expected to see this failure of a man ever again, least of all in his office. He watched as Faraz left. Then he watched in astonishment as Jamal waited for Faraz to pass. Jamal's head remained lowered and he followed carefully a few steps behind Faraz. When they were a good distance away Mohammed opened his desk and pulled out something and ran after the two. Mohammed could not contain himself anymore, he shouted out so that the whole office could hear him, "Jamal!"

Faraz and Jamal stopped halfway but didn't turn around.

Mohammed walked straight up to Jamal. He was still shocked to see how Jamal was dressed in a ripped and dirty kurta. Sandals instead of dress shoes. His hands were calloused and his skin was dry.

Jamal was scared and nearly trembling, but he would receive no pity.

Mohammed grabbed his hand and placed something in it. He made sure Jamal was looking at him. Although his eyes shed a light of purity from his fear Mohammed's message was unchanged. He leaned into Jamal's ear and whispered, "Next time finish what you started." Mohammed then spit on the floor next to Jamal's feet and walked back to his office. He could have done more. He could have but didn't want to further aggravate his stance with Faraz, even though this was probably the reason he waited for Jamal.

Jamal opened his hands to a cement rock, and just like the life he had led to that point it began to crumble in his hands.

"Jamal, come. You have to get the car." Faraz commanded as he walked to the elevator. He didn't turn around and just walked out of the office.

Jamal just stood in the hall and watched pieces of his former life fall to the floor.

22

The reception was the largest thing Karachi had seen in quite some time. It even rivaled the gatherings thrown by the prime minister. It was a rare event to be held in the name of humanity. However it was as brilliant as the Ahmed family had imagined anything done in their father's name would be. The search lights out front brought unwanted attention, as did everything else present inside the reception hall. It was a welcome and farewell party. Its guest ranged from all ages and all walks of life. It was the event of the year that many Pakistani's looked forward to, at least for the past three years since its inception. It was the event that decided which person would be worthy of carrying Pakistan's name to the convention in Islambad.

Time was kind to the people arriving for traffic had been diverted just so the honored guests would have a shot at being on time. The entrance to the hall was an elongated covered tent that extended to the street. Cars pulled up to and about from the hall. People were emptied out and then shuffled into the hall. Families were dressed in fancy outfits, some matching some not. Sons followed in the footsteps of their fathers while daughters followed behind the mothers who were far behind.

That is not how Mohammed saw his family being portrayed. He walked with them proudly and confident that each member of his family was as proud to walk with him. With his wife in arm he held the hand of his daughter Neeloofur as they walked down the isle. All the children were excited to be with their father. Rehan was the only one not holding the others hands. Even though he was the youngest he was forced to mature much quicker than the rest of his siblings.

Mohammed was bracing for meeting people and seeing faces that he had already rid out of his mind. He made only a small amount of friends and even more enemies through his way of planning. Although each man he denied would greet him with a smile, their hearts and minds were filled with moans and aches. Still Mohammed would walk amongst them and still he would be the one being honored.

Each family was seated around lavish tables outlined with candles and suspended below separate chandeliers. Mohammed had already made up his mind that he would not leave his families side. If someone wanted to meet him, they would have to do it within the secure limitations of his family.

Mohammed and his family were seated on and elongated table next to the right side of a podium on an elevated stage. From there they could see each person peer at them as they entered the enormous hall. Among the setting on the table was a frame and small pamphlet listed with all the achievements of the men being honored today. Although Mohammed's achievements were not as long as the others listed, he was amid the most dubious.

As his family was still getting situated he listened to his children comment on each person as they entered. They would wave when aunts and uncles entered the hall. They would smile once a family friend would openly wave back.

Much to Mohammed's amazement, people were showing up on time. Also to his surprise Faraz and his entourage were seated far and away from Mohammed. It did not go unnoticed as more men were lined up to greet Faraz than were taking their seats. Faraz and Jamal stood in the corner of the hall smiling and laughing, greeting and shaking the hands of many of Mohammed's guests.

It didn't matter to Mohammed he was surrounded by his own entourage. Mohammed looked at his wife, still so young and beautiful. She was surrounded by the knowledge that her marriage defined her. Then he looked at his two daughters to his far right - Shehla and Neeloofur. They were ready to begin their journey into college and maybe even marriage, and they would not be denied the education their mother was. He looked to his far left and saw his other daughters Duree and Zarina, so smart and so daring, he was both proud and afraid of the attention they were receiving. Then he patted his son on the back. Rehan was the only one standing with him and waiting until the guests had been seated. He was about to enter into his teens yet he held a presence similar to his father's. He was young and still had so much to learn about this world. Still he held a respect that was ascribed to him from birth. In the middle of them all was Mohammed their provider. As much as his family loved him for what he had provided for them, they needed his presence more than anything. It provided them with stability and motivation, warmth and refinement.

There was something about tonight that Mohammed was excited about. It wasn't the first time he had been honored. He couldn't put his finger on it, all he could do was listen to the voice in families eyes and hope for the best. He had only told them hours ago of his plans to travel to Islamabad, and the extended time he would be away from them. They were under the impression that the convention was only to be a few days. He knew they hated to be away from him, but he couldn't stand to bare them the news and see pieces of their heart shed away.

"Ladies and Gentlemen." An announcer snuck his way onto the stage and spoke into the microphone. It was the oddest thing to see a loud scurrying crowd silenced with three words. "Please take your seats and dinner will be served accordingly." Perhaps those were the words that the crowd was waiting to hear. The crowd immediately hurried to their seats and quieted down as waiters meandered through seas of tables serving and cleaning.

"Are all these people here for your Abu?" The silence gave Rehan a chance to speak with his father.

"Not for me, for us." Mohammed pointed from one end of the stage to the other. "They are here to see us honored."

"Do they plan was well?"

"Yes but in a different manner."

"What do they do?"

"Well you know that I plan the city and the streets, and I pass any requests for buildings like mosques and schools and offices. Well that man down there plans shelters for the poor and special programs for the children. And the man down a little farther built a road that stretches all the way to Lahore and from Lahore it will spread until Islamabad."

"But what you do is more important than what they do, I know it. Everyone talks about how great you are and all the things you do for the love of Pakistan. That makes you better than those people. Right?"

"Better is not the right word. I am just receiving an award for the gift I was given."

"Doesn't that make you better?"

"No. I am just using my abilities to help other people."

"But if you have an ability that no one else has, doesn't that make you better than other people?

Mohammed was never ready to hear those words come out of his son's mouth. Is this what he thought of his father? He had grown so large that the idea of his father was larger than Karachi. He pulled Rehan in closer, "What I do is for Karachi and Pakistan, that is it. There is nothing greater in this world than doing something with the pure intention of your heart. I don't do it to be recognized or to get large amounts of money."

"But you do get both of those things, right? Aren't all these people here to see you and to please you? Don't you like being around these people? Isn't it great to see them jealous?

Mohammed didn't know how to answer his question, he sighed and looked at his son who was waiting for his response. "Rehan, God blesses men with the gifts to help those who don't have the same abilities. What he didn't give anyone is the ability to outgrow themselves. It is like a bird building its nest or growing its wings. It will not build more than what is necessary and it will not grow its wings farther than it can stretch. I build only what is necessary and take what I have earned. Anything beyond that is greed. The shadows we cast can never be larger than what we are." He took a tighter hold of his son. "God gave each man and woman a mind so that they can make decisions for themselves. But you have to be careful not to fill your mind with delusions. That is when we fail this life. Do you understand?"

Rehan shook his head and before Mohammed could clarify his response. A waiter interrupted them to set their plates. Rehan was pulled out of his father's address and into the delicious smell that rubbed his senses.

Mohammed watched and envied how easy it was for his son to ignore the tests and trials in this life. His innocence was the calm that the entire hall should have dumped onto their plates to taste. Instead he looked at the guests below and saw how they gorged in the absence of light. They were a flock of sheep that waited for the grass to grow and wool to be shed. Mohammed was not the shepherd, he was time that pushed forward seasons.

The night passed and accolades were passed out. Mohammed reached for his plaque and shared in the moment with his family. There were smiles and laughs, handshakes and hugs. Pictures were taken. Pictures that most likely would be looked upon once then discarded. Mohammed once again was forced to pretend that he enjoyed the company of his denied proposal guests. The lights in the hall were dimmed to project the pictures of Mohammed and other guest's works upon a great wall. Oooh's and aaah's became the symphony that accompanied each picture. It was after that point that Mohammed was given his gift of representation. He shared it with the other guests on stage and took it back to his family. He showed it to his family who, as he had suspected, were not as thrilled to see his invitation to Islamabad. For him it was an honor, for his family it meant nearing a time without Mohammed. Their compassion was genuine while their smiles were not. The only thing Mohammed could do was wait until his time in Islamabad passed to regain their hearts.

Although the trip was several weeks away he could already sense his families thoughts of him being a stranger. Mohammed held onto the plaque and peered at his reflection through the engraved words. It seemed that every accomplishment he received, he received alone.

23

There was no denying the pain anymore. A hammer was pounded against Mohammed's forehead with each passing moment. His mouth would mix from being in a dry spell to being uncontrollably salivating. Anything Mohammed would grab would have the imprint of his hand from the sweat pouring out of it. For the second time in his life he was truly afraid. Nothing had prepared him for this moment. He sat and thought that if he could just hold out until morning the pain would simply fade with time. Noises would enter his head. He thought he heard voices, then the water in the bathroom running. He could swear he heard the phone ring. He picked it up.

"Hello, who is there?" He put down the phone and stared at it waiting to catch it ringing again. He trembled his fingers in anticipation of the next ring. He was like a vulture carefully stalking a dead carcass. Then all of a sudden there was a knock on the door. He jumped out of bed and ran to the door, like he had never run for anything in his life. He opened it to see that there was nothing and no one there. His suspicions of this entire floor being practically empty were becoming true. He shut it and locked it, then peered in the peephole once again. He crawled back to the base of the bed and didn't have the strength to pull himself up. Suddenly a stabbing pain in the midst of his chest caused him to cry out in pain. It was like a pair of scissors being forced into his heart and then being pulled open and twisted. It was so excruciating that his nails broke from scratching the floor. He could hear the blood rush throughout his body, it was not a good sign. He reached for the phone but the line came back empty.

"Help me." He cried over and over again as loud as he could, but the room remained empty and dark. He then made his way back to the phone and dropped it to the floor. The receiver bounced its way into his hands. He continually pressed the hotel operator key waiting for someone.

"Front desk." Finally a voice.

"Please help me, I need an ambulance." Mohammed cried over the phone.

"I apologize sir no one can get in or out of the hotel sir the entrance is blocked. We could send a doctor."

"I need someone please!"

"Yes of course! We do have a doctor on staff here. Your room number sir?"

Mohammed couldn't think. Every thought that came out of his mind now was filled with pain. He cried out in pain over the phone.

"Sir your room number." The voice tried to hurry him.

"I don't know, I'm on the top floor, just send someone!"

He hung up the phone and crawled to the window to see the entry was blocking anyone from entering or exiting. It seemed like the entire crowd outside in the courtyard was nearly everyone from inside the hotel. The fire had engulfed and whole car. People stood around and tried to help but were being waved off by the hospital staff. Mohammed pounded his fist as hard as he could against the glass. He even yelled. Nothing. Even if he was heard no one was going to turn their attention away from the fire. He couldn't wait any longer, he had to try to get somewhere on his own.

"I can get to the elevator." He began speaking out loud to himself. "No, it's no use, too many people are using it." He doubted himself and his plan. "What about the stairs?" He would surely hurt himself further trying to get down one flight of those stairs. "Why is this happening? Think, you fool, what did you do to render yourself so helpless?" Mohammed thought about his lunch, was his food improperly cooked? "No, that couldn't be it. What else did I have today? Oh my God, the tea..."

His eyes could not focus upon anything. His toes arrested without his power. His mouth began to develop foam that he spewed around him. His chest locked up and fingers formed stiff behind his back. His head hit the ground hard. The only thing he could express now were his thoughts. He watched as a stream of blood formed in front of his left eye and crept down the floor. When he blinked his eye would fill with that very same blood.

It mixed with the foam that snuck out of his mouth. Although he could no longer control it, his body began to spasm with his head remaining in the same place, in a pool of his own fluids. His gritted his teeth so hard that he felt a few of them break in his mouth. His continually hard breathing sucked in the pool of blood and blew out at mixture of the same but outlined with misty saliva. Every part of his body was out of his control now except for his mind, which could still feel the unexplainable pain he felt through each bone, muscle, joint, limb, and hair. After the brief episode, which seemed as if it lasted for a lifetime, Mohammed lay still on the floor. The occasional twitch followed by the loud, slow beat of his heart brought an ounce of life. Mohammed closed his eyes and prayed for any kind of peace. Through the twitching and beating his whole head was now under the bed in complete darkness. A sudden violent spasm caused him to hit the back of his head extremely hard against the leg of the bed. And just like that the peace he prayed for came. Random thoughts came in and out of his head. He had an eternity of darkness. No longer did he hurt. To his horror and comfort he could not feel anything. He was broken, half under the bed, almost speechless, and still he managed to embrace his tranquility. He finally had the moments of his life in his mind all to himself.

He woke up in his bed next to Sophia. She was lying and smiling, neither of them saying a word, just holding the stunning view of each other in their eyes. Everything that could be said had been said, they were just relishing in the fact that nothing new needed be said. He hoped that she knew how much he loved her. Like a puppet he was pulled from the bed into the sky while she just lay there looking in the same direction, a direction without Mohammed.

The sounds of small horns and balloons popping outlined his family centered at one of Rehans' birthday parties. There was not one sad face in the crowd as Rehan struggled mightily to cut through the enormous cake. He saw his daughters running around and playing with the other children. His wife was dressed in a sari that he had just bought her. No one seemed to notice Mohammed in the corner alone. Yet they all continued. The door next to Mohammed opened and like a vacuum he was sucked out of his home. He saw the boards pull off the house and windows shatter as they too were being pulled with him. Into a void of light he was cast and into a sea of doubt he swam.

The sea washed back and forth as his mother and father were swinging Mohammed like a child. Their steps were imprinted in the once clean shoreline. However, with each step and swing, his footprints landed into cement. The water would empty itself into his family's prints yet only theirs would wash away and disappear. Mohammed looked behind him to the edge of the beach. He could see all of his steps were still stuck in the sand. His father looked back with him and looked at Noor. They both let go of Mohammed and continued down the beach. Mohammed stood there afraid to take another step. He sat and waited for the tide to come in and sweep him into oblivion. There sun quickly turned to moon and the water was now at Mohammed's throat. It engulfed him after a few waves but did not bother to take his footprints.

In his old home in Hyderabad, Abdullah was sitting next to the servants entry on the side of the kitchen. He waved to Mohammed and signaled for him to join him outside. A boy with stronger legs, Mohammed raced out to catch Abdullah. He jumped out on the cement and landed in Abdullah's shadow. Abdullah handed him a cricket bat and ran to the other side of the lot. Mohammed was still in his shadow. Abdullah stopped and without warning threw a hardened ball quickly in Mohammed's direction. Mohammed lifted his bat without swinging and felt the ball smack the flat side and escape the courtyard and into the air. Mohammed stood watching the ball travel endlessly into the sky while Abdullah walked up to him and looked down upon him. Abdullah's shadow had now completely covered Mohammed entirely and began to wrap around him like a heavy blanket. He was swallowed into a darkened abyss, with no light to escape with.

Mohammed brought himself back to his unmovable self. He had almost twitched himself to the bathroom. Still he could not voluntarily move and still he could not feel the pain. He heard men shuffle at his door and try to open the lock. He would have to wait for he could not open it. As long as there was no pain he tried telling himself everything would be fine. He focused all his energy on whisking his mind into a mysterious wonderland.

Rolling green hills and white powder topped the mountains in the distance and a fog settled in between a dome of Islamabad the city of Karachi. The sea was to his left. Mohammed was perched on top of a hill overlooking the entire land of Pakistan. Each of her beautiful features were towering above the landscape. Above it all it seemed was Mohammed. He saw her rivers cut the land and he could see the barren land extend into the distance. There was only him and his Pakistan. How her beauty was beyond anything he could imagine to ever seeing again. He felt her heart beat with all his senses. The sun to his back, the moon to his front and the stars were aligned above. Each asset of the land was within his reach, yet he was afraid to disturb any of her beauty. He could taste her heaven and feel the burn of her hell. He closed his eyes and whispered to himself. With all his might he wished and with all his might he wondered. It was something he had whispered many times before. Something he had learned and passed onto his children. Something he hoped his children would pass on to their children. Then he opened eyes and looked at the land. Nothing.